Z Plague Book 1

Homeless City

"Z Genesis"

It's fiction. Have fun!

"Z Plague Series"
Book 1

Homeless City

"Z Genesis"

By D. R. Swan

Book Cover Image By
Evan

(HC022alt)

Dedication

To Evan and Ryan, always foremost in my thoughts and prayers.

Acknowledgments

Thanks to everyone for their help, support, and kindness. No one accomplishes anything alone. Special thanks to Evan, Donna, Fred, and Blair for their help over and above.

Preface

And the dead shall rise...

Long Beach, California

Late Spring, 2036

Scratching, then scratching again... Low scratching... Muffled...

Long Beach's Coroner, David Meltzer, turned his head.

Mice?

Not a good thing in here, he thought.

He took off his wire-rimmed glasses and cleaned the lenses with a tissue then went back to his clipboard and checked the notes that had arrived with the last stiff. A man lay on a gurney in a body bag in his forties who died after walking out in front of a bus...

Dumb ass...

Meltzer read the notes. Most of the bones in the guy's body were broken or cracked. Severe internal injuries... Open skull. Brain matter outside of the cranium...

More scratching...

Meltzer looked up then glanced back down at a corpse on his stainless-steel table, a woman he was working on who died mysteriously in her sixties. He had her chest opened and had taken some samples for toxicology. The results should be back shortly. In examining her organs, he thought she shouldn't be dead. Heart good... other organs normal, even above average. She was found in her home by a relative. Only been dead for a few hours before her discovery. There had been a respiratory illness that had recently sprung up in Long Beach making a lot of people sick and overwhelming some of the emergency rooms. He thought that this may have been the reason for the woman's demise. Toxicology might find something. Could be some kind of virus or bacteria.

"Odd," he thought aloud. Stitch her up and move on to the next one... Bagged and tagged... "Into the freezer, Ma'am."

Scratching...

"What—is— that?"

He turned his ear to try to figure out the direction of the noise.

Finishing with the woman, Meltzer slid her back into her freezer compartment.

A bang as if something metallic was struck. It sounded as though it came from one of the other freezer compartments.

Meltzer walked over to the bank of stacked cabinets. There was some kind of movement in compartment A6. He raised his eyes and thought it might be postmortem muscle contraction. He slid open the compartment. The compartment was low and he had to bend down to peer inside. A hand reached out and grasped his throat. It was cat-quick and it gripped like a vise. He struggled then blackness filled his vision from the edges...

“Z Genesis”

Homeless City

Part 1

The Day America Died...

Chapter 1

November 2032

Three-and-a-half years earlier...

The election results were surprising. Though constant corruption was uncovered in his administration, and a poor showing in the polls, the aging, incumbent, President of the United States, Donald Fergusson, was narrowly reelected to a second term.

The next morning, his Press Secretary was on all the morning news shows claiming that despite a continual smear campaign, the American people had spoken, though his narrow electoral college win was overshadowed by the fact that he lost the popular vote by nearly 4,000,000 votes.

Emboldened by his victory, Fergusson began replacing competent members of his cabinet with yes men and loyalists which allowed him to get away with increasingly corrupt policies. The key replacement was the current Attorney General who Fergusson sacked then replaced with Gilbert Price, an under-qualified partisan with no compunction to allow the President to use him as his own personal attorney and prosecutor.

As a result, Fergusson began using the Justice Department to attack his political enemies. The opposition party became outraged at the blatant attacks on members of their party but the President found that instead of condemnation, he became more popular with his constituents. It was the inverse of rational and would be the beginning of a constant attack on trusted institutions just as Hitler had accomplished in the 1930s.

As it was, America had deteriorated under Fergusson's leadership in the past four years both economically and culturally as his constant divisive use of inflammatory rhetoric deeply divided the country. The prospect of the country's continued decline was a near certainty.

Internationally, Fergusson had alienated most of America's staunchest allies and had spent some time coddling its enemies. It seemed that he was most interested in furthering his own interests rather than the countries.

With alliances fragile, most of the United States' allies began pulling back on sharing intelligence and several trade wars between the EU and the United States escalated the tensions.

Those rich American's who were leaders in their industries and technologies became increasingly concerned at a gradual and observable loss of the rule of law and freedom of the people of America, so they had begun to slowly move their families, residences, and their corporate headquarters from the United States to Germany, Canada, France, Great Britain, and even as far away as Australia and New Zealand, though not officially announcing that anything had changed in either case. As America continued to decline as a result of the President's corrupt policies, these corporate leaders limited their time in the United States and began setting up manufacturing in other countries in case the American economy collapsed. Most were already global corporations but the industrial leaders taking their wealth and families out of the United States was becoming a national embarrassment. President Fergusson barely noticed being wrapped in his own corruption.

Chapter 2

October 1, 2033

Towards the end of the first year of Fergusson's reelection, the economy collapsed. This event was easily predictable as the free market became replaced with corruption and graft that started from the top. The dollar which at one time had been the most stable currency in the world began to rapidly lose its value. Prices then began rising as anything imported became increasingly expensive. The stock market lost thirty percent of its value in a week.

President Fergusson and America were increasingly becoming internationally isolated as usually trusted allies of the United States, the remaining world's great democracies, continued distancing themselves from America and would no longer purchase American bonds to fund the enormous deficits run up by the President and his administration. Interest rates soared bringing about the worst of scenarios of a collapsing economy and spiking interest rates.

Because the wealthiest, brightest, and most innovative from American society had already fled the increasingly unpredictable, lawless, and chaotic United States, taking their wealth and relocating where they could find freedom and the rule of law, they and their wealth were safe from the turmoil, but millions of working Americans were thrown out of work in the near-collapse and lost everything.

The Russians and the Chinese offered to buy the unwanted American bonds to fund the exploding deficits but put strings on their purchases that allowed them to be free of prior restrictions.

As a result, Taiwan was the first country to fall, taken over by the Chinese.

America made no protest but closed down its semiconductor and high-tech factories located there, hoping that the Chinese could not steal the technology. The Americans were too late and the Chinese were able to steal it anyway.

Next, Ukraine was usurped by the Russians.

America was silent.

Both China and Russia were expanding with no one to halt their imperialism.

The European Union screamed in protest in the United Nations knowing that Russia would soon expand in their direction.

America again had no comment and was collapsing from within. With utter lawlessness in the White House, it was difficult to expect the population to be law-abiding. All violent crime soared.

Because not everyone in the Secret Service was loyal to the President and his corrupt regime, some uncovered plots of assassination would not be reported and politicians would die. The country was in chaos. Rioters flooded the streets. These protests were first peaceful but soon became violent.

As a result, Fergusson then created a new police force that combined America's Secret Services, state and local police departments, the military, and the

FBI. This new federalized force would be called the Citizen Guard and began showing up on the streets in black and forest green camo with CG monikered red armbands. They wore helmets, body armor, sported bad attitudes, and began putting down the riots with overwhelming force.

In the next months to follow, millions of Americans were cast out of their homes. Bankruptcies skyrocketed and Fergusson's friends and associates became owners of nearly all of the distressed real estate in the country, paying pennies on the dollar, and having no attack of conscience when it came to evicting and throwing people into the streets.

A New York Times headline read: *"Homelessness out of control! Hordes descend onto the L.A. basin."*

The article began: *"Today, another ten thousand people entered L.A. on a steady stream that crossed the Grapevine in a procession of people on foot, some pushing shopping carts..."*

The article finished with, *"...The President will be addressing the Nation with his plan to rescue the homeless!"*

Fergusson took to the airwaves saying that his administration was formulating a plan to help the cities with the homeless situation and would put his ideas before congress in the near future. The statement was purposely vague but the President assured the American people that, "They would soon see an improvement in their towns and neighborhoods."

Both Houses of Congress met in private session to discuss the President's plan which was to build a large city specifically for the homeless, a place where the homeless would be taken by force. Some members raised concerns at the suggestion, claiming that it would infringe on the rights of the people who were homeless, a right that they couldn't care less about. But like everything in the changing American Government, caring about the rights of Americans was just a show. Congress, though, would secretly pledge one trillion dollars to establish "*Homeless City.*" It was important to Fergusson that any word of this plan was to be kept under wraps. His popularity in the polls had sunk to a dismal 17 percent approval rating and he didn't want to be painted with an, "*internment camp,*" brush.

The next problem that they faced was where to build this secret, sprawling, thirty-square-mile institution. To call it a city was a bit of a stretch.

Fergusson had no desire for the public to know the details of this idea and deferred the decisions to the counsel of Governors due to meet next month to address the problem.

Chapter 3

Boulder, Colorado

Council of Governors

March 29, 2034

The Governor of California, Roy Blackburn, stood on the podium in front of the other forty-nine Governors of the states of America, and ready to address the attendees.

The room was small with just the Governors and two of Fergusson's observers allowed to attend. The two observers stood at the sides of the podium to have a good view of the seated Governors. No reporters were allowed, no aids, or support staff, just the Governors, and the contents and comments made in this meeting were supposed to be kept strictly confidential.

Blackburn began his statement: "California's cities are being overwhelmed. You have all been apprised of President Fergusson's plan to build a *Homeless City*. I propose that we go ahead with the idea without delay and build it in California because we have the largest homeless population."

Blackburn stepped back from the podium and pulled out a large easel with several large artist's renderings of a sprawling, advanced city.

"Here, by Death Valley is where I propose to place the city."

Voices of agreement rose from the seated Governors because they knew that Blackburn was President Fergusson's man and that this plan came directly from the President. No one wanted to be seen as negative.

Governor Blackburn continued, "This is not going to be a prison. It will be a state-of-the-art, fully mechanized city with a complete subway system, specialized housing, vocational training, and individual healthcare. Most of the people living in the city will hopefully be transitioned out at some point. Some of this problem began when we stopped taking care of people who clearly could not take care of themselves, long before President Donald Fergusson's great leadership. A large portion of the city will take care of those who cannot survive in society because of various reasons."

Blackburn turned over pictures on the easel and showed the concept pictures of the site.

He continued, "This portion will be for the drug and alcohol addicted and where they will receive care. Most of the people living in the city will have small jobs that they will not be paid for. Their work will be considered payment for their housing, food, and medical care. Once the doctors and administrators conclude that the people have sufficiently reached a level of being able to take care of themselves, they will be relocated to a place of their choosing and allowed to live in a halfway house for a specified length of time to be established later."

Some discussion arose from the governors at that but then quieted.

Blackburn waited patiently then continued, "I realize that this is going to be controversial, but this problem cannot continue to plague our cities and it's going to get worse. The economy has taken another leg down which means more people out of work and thrown from their homes. We need to act now. I propose locating this city in California because I know that no one wants it in their own backyard. The site that I have chosen is far away from any other cities, close to an old abandoned military base where there is still some infrastructure to house the construction workers and engineers who will be tasked to build the city. It will take an army of workers to complete it quickly but this will employ a large amount of the workers who are now out of work or who will soon be losing their jobs. That's all I have for now. We can discuss more of the details when we break up into our groups. Thanks."

There was no surprise that applause broke out among the governors. Blackburn knew that they had all been pressured. The devil, however, as always, was going to be in the details.

Blackburn had stepped away from the podium, but he turned and stepped back. He tapped the microphone to get the governor's attention who had begun talking amongst themselves. They all glanced back at the podium.

Blackburn began again, "Let me remind you that this is to be kept a complete secret. If the homeless begin finding out about it, they might become harder to round up. Also, this new city is not optional for the homeless. They will be forcibly removed from their encampments and off the streets so we can clean up our cities. I don't think we want the public at large to know of this, either. We don't want a reoccurrence of large demonstrations of people protesting this policy."

Blackburn stepped away again from the podium and the other Governors stood and began to mill around. The sound of murmuring rose in the room.

Chapter 4

April 16, 2034

The decision of the Governors didn't take long. Once Homeless City was approved and the construction companies were chosen, the construction would begin without delay. All of the paperwork and blueprints had been done in advance and once the final location was agreed upon, the work would immediately begin. No environmental impact reports and no pulling permits, there was no time to waste. The city would be built on the floor of an old dried lakebed in the Death Valley region of Southern California. It was away from the small towns and cities that sparsely dotted the parched land. There was only one road in and one road out. A small secret military base had been located there over 100 years prior but had been abandoned in the 1940s. There were rumors that it had housed alien wreckage long before the infamous Area 51 had become popularized. Below the old base was a labyrinth of tunnels.

Homeless City would be built adjacent to the base so the construction workers could use the dilapidated barracks for storage and a place to sleep and eat while sequestered until the city was functional.

May 29, 2034

An army of workers descended into the hot, dry region with a convoy of heavy vehicles to begin the work. Homeless City was to be a sprawling city, built one story with no high-rising buildings. The only buildings of more than one story would be the induction centers, the security buildings, and towers that would monitor the entire city using sophisticated video and sensors. The city, when completed, could house one million of the homeless and would have underground transportation and storage facilities. The current plans were to have it not be gated, though it would be surrounded by a fence in case the Government wanted to lock it down, but it was thought that no one would try to walk out. The city was surrounded by brutal desert in all directions and though it was theoretically possible that someone might be able to survive the walk out, it would be a monumental task. In all directions, the nearest towns were more than fifty miles away, a fact that would be shared with all who would be residing in the new, remote Homeless City.

The work began, raising clouds of lakebed dust high into the sky as earthmoving equipment gouged out the underground infrastructure for the first phase of the city. Estimated time for the cities unveiling, 18 months. The city at that time would not be complete but would begin receiving the homeless. As the city expanded, more homeless would be relocated there as the housing increased.

Part 2

Hanna Scott...

Chapter 5

Los Angeles, California

November 7, 2035

29-year-old, Hanna Scott had become successful. By any measure, she had been living the American dream at a time when that dream was fading. She had graduated from UCLA, a business major specializing in social media, just three years before and had landed a job in advertising with the prestigious Warton Agency.

The agency was one of the most influential in the world with branches in Los Angeles, New York City, London, and Hong Kong.

Hanna was not tall at five-three with pale skin. She was lean and fit with kind, blue eyes, and thick, dirty blond hair that laid upon her shoulders. Her nose was freckly and her smile was warm and wholesome and would put even the most skeptical person in her presence at ease.

She had done well and in business was driven to succeed.

She grew up in foster care. Her parents had passed away in a car accident when she was but two. She had been pulled from that car while it burned.

Hanna had no other family. She had to work her way through school and sometimes had two jobs so it took her an additional two years to graduate.

Through school, she had not made many friends, though, everyone who knew her felt as though she was their friend. She had a way of making those around her feel comfortable as if they were family.

Her best friend, Francine Wallace, died tragically two years prior in a robbery gone bad at a convenience store. She had been shot in the chest, nicking an artery, and had bled to death on the store's floor.

So, Hanna was virtually alone in the world, but she had landed this great job, was excelling at it, and was on her way up.

The fact that Hanna did not have many friends was an insight into her psychology and she knew it. She had been married at an early age while in college and she loved her husband but continually found the need to stray. In their three-year marriage, she had been with four men on the side. One in particular who she thought was the perfect man for her, but he was married also and ended their illicit affair. She had lost touch with him and wondered how he was doing. He had a young child back then. Hanna's marriage ended badly.

Her second marriage lasted just five months when she had strayed and got caught. Her husband gave her an ultimatum asking her if she honestly would promise not to stray again but she said that she just couldn't promise that. So, the marriage predictably ended.

The last good relationship that she had been in was with Mike Branch. He was kind. She had fallen in love with him and moved into his apartment. He was talking about marriage just after dating for four months. But Hanna was simultaneously becoming restless and predictably began another affair that sabotaged the relationship. She began seeing a man that she had met in college. Her boyfriend found out, of course, and ended the relationship to her relief.

One of the men that Hanna had seen for a short time in her dalliances was Jack Morgan. He was also restless and was in the military and had told Hanna that he reenlisted to go back to another war-torn region. He explained to Hanna that he was not happy unless he was someplace where the adrenalin was coursing through his veins. When he left, Hanna was upset for weeks. Since, he had never left her thoughts.

Afterward, Hanna had been in several short-term relationships. She was currently seeing Ian McCaffery, who seemed more like herself. He was her new boss, never a good idea, and ten years her senior. For the last three months, they had been dating exclusively and things stayed at a comfortably shallow level. For some reason, she hadn't felt that need to stray. The relationship was working.

One night after Hanna had finished work, she went to Ian's penthouse overlooking the L.A. skyline. He had informed her that he was going to have a small party with some friends. The Saturday before they had both gone to a Halloween party, where dressed in costumes, they danced, ate, and had a great time.

Hanna arrived late and the party, which had begun without her, was in full swing and seemed to be filled with people who were also equally as shallow as Ian with no one there seeming to care in the least if everyone in the place dropped dead. There was nearly an equal number of women and men and all were obviously successful. A slight haze of cannabis smoke hung in the air. Floor-to-ceiling windows lined the open-concept living room/dining room/kitchen area giving a nearly 180-degree view. Gas flames burnt in an expansive fireplace. It was breathtaking.

That night would become enlightening. Hanna found out that her man, Ian, had a concealed kink.

Ian was smashed and was dancing in the middle of the room alone. His salt and pepper hair was a bit disheveled and his clothes were rumpled with his white shirt half-unbuttoned and untucked.

Hanna had never seen him like that before. He had always seemed as though he wouldn't allow a hair out of place when out or around people.

Hanna strode to Ian and hugged him. He got her a glass of wine and they mingled as Ian introduced her around. The talk was mostly about money and business and intensely dry.

Two hours passed and the party began to thin. Several people said their goodbyes and left. A friend of Ian's lit a joint and passed it to Hanna. A mirror lay on a coffee table with a razor blade and lines of powder waiting to be snorted. Hanna took a drag of the joint then snorted a line on the mirror. The friend of Ian's that she was sitting next to was far past sober and he openly flirted with her as they shared the joint and cocaine. Ian had wandered off chatting as the guests of the party continued to leave.

By 1:15 am most of the guests had left. Every person who had not gone home was drunk or high or both. Hanna was feeling no pain. When she closed her eyes, the room spun slightly.

Several people left in the room continued to party and dance.

Hanna glimpsed Ian from across the room. He had a wild look in his eyes and he walked back to her, took a drag from the joint she was sharing, and pulled her off the couch where she was sitting close to the guy sharing his weed. She was deep into her third glass of wine and had needed to push the guy's hand from her thigh several times.

Ian said with a slight slur, "Dance with me."

She smiled and nodded and put her arms on Ian's shoulders.

He began to run his hands up and down Hanna's body on her hips and across her backside.

"God, I love this body," Ian slurred.

Hanna glanced at his intense eyes and smiled though she thought his wandering hands were a bit too intimate for the party, even though by this time, most of the people had left.

Ian reached over and dimmed the lights in the room, then brought Hanna back to himself and continued to slowly dance with her. His hands again traced the contours of her body sliding under her blouse and pushing up one of the cups of her bra. He held her breast, stroking the nipple which rose to him.

She looked around uncomfortably but could feel her arousal. Several of the people left in the room had taken notice and smiled in their direction. She brought her hand up and covered his, trying to hide its wandering.

"Ian, come on, stop," she whispered unconvincingly and she smiled playfully but her unease was rising.

He chuckled.

She pushed his hand down a bit and they danced. She again glanced around.

What she saw was that the other people remaining in the room were also, now a bit more intimate than she thought would be normal for a party of this kind. Their attention had moved away from Ian and herself. The guy she had shared the joint with was still on the couch, now with another woman. Like the couples remaining, they were kissing and their hands were exploring.

Hanna began not to just feel uncomfortable but that something was very wrong.

She was aroused by Ian, though. She always had been. He had this power. She turned her attention back to him. His hand again was on her breast. She weakly pushed it down again just a bit.

"Later," she whispered, thinking that it was just too much alcohol and the drugs clouding his better judgment. She had finished her third glass of wine and had set down the glass. She could feel the room begin to spin.

"Oh," she slurred, "I'm thrashed."

Ian chuckled.

She could hear clapping behind her as she pushed Ian's wandering hand again from her breast. She turned to see a woman dancing as if she were about to undress.

At first, Hanna laughed and thought that the woman was just clowning around but then she began unbuttoning her blouse.

Hanna's eyes widened in shock.

Ian smiled broadly.

Everyone left in the room, except for Hanna, but including Ian, began to clap and exhort the woman to continue.

The woman smiled shyly but had no mixed feelings about continuing and she let her blouse fall to the floor.

Hanna was stunned as the woman closed her eyes and slowly danced, and as she did so, each piece of clothing remaining on her slim body also ended up on the floor at her feet.

There were only eight people now in the room with everyone else having left.

The woman dancing had reached the point where she was only dressed in skin as she had removed her bra last, letting it slip from her hand and drift to the floor. She danced seductively in a way that made you want to watch. It wasn't lude. It was subtle and mesmerizing.

The woman smiled at Hanna and her eyes beckoned Hanna to join her.

Hanna knew where this party was going. She couldn't believe it and she turned to Ian who was watching with rapt attention.

Hanna whispered, "Ian, what the hell's going on?"

"Just watch," he replied quietly, not glancing her way.

A second woman joined the first and danced, also removing her clothes. A third woman sat with eyes wide and like Hanna, shocked at the turn that the party had taken. The man who had brought her whispered to her to join the two unclothed women. She shook her head no but he whispered something in her ear and she reluctantly stood.

The two women who were dancing smiled.

The expression on the third woman's face was revealing enough to have an idea of what her boss had told her. She reluctantly removed her clothes.

The man who was with the shy woman stood and walked to her, taking her in his arms, and began to slow dance. He ran his hands over the back of her body and whispered, "This is your way up."

The two other men who were watching stood then and walked to the two other women who were dancing together and began to slow dance with them. The dancing between the two experienced couples was becoming more intimate as the women and men allowed their hands to freely roam each other's bodies. The shy woman was still completely reluctant and danced stiffly with her man.

The three men dancing stopped and turned to Hanna and began clapping for her to join in and also remove her clothes.

She looked like the proverbial deer in the headlights.

The two experienced nude women then strolled over to Hanna, pulling her away from Ian, and began encouraging her to dance. She shook her head no.

Disappointment was clearly displayed on the women's faces.

Ian walked to Hanna, took her hands, and pulled her away from the two women and to the side of the room. He embraced her then whispered in her ear, "Come on, let's have some fun."

"Fun?"

"Yeah, fun. This will be a night that you won't ever forget."

He turned her to watch the goings-on in the room, hugging her from behind.

Hanna realized the obvious, this was not your typical party. She briefly had lost track of what Ian was up to as the room spun from the alcohol and drugs as she observed the surreal scene. Two of the three couples had moved together onto the couch, their bodies entwined. The shy woman was with the man who brought her on a chair also engaged in foreplay.

Hanna turned her head back to Ian who had started to unbutton her blouse. She thought that maybe she could redirect Ian's attention.

She turned to face him and suggested, "Let's slip away."

"No," Ian said and he became more aggressive.

Hanna glanced back around at the couples all now mostly nude. They had moved from foreplay to full-on sex. The room was spinning in the smokey haze. Hanna felt disoriented, very drunk, and very high.

She still thought that she could get control of the situation and she said, "Ian, this isn't for me. I, I mean, I'm not comfortable with this."

Ian didn't respond. His expression was stern and he unbuttoned her blouse further.

She crossed her arms over her front.

"I don't want to do this," she slurred unconvincingly.

Ian appeared disgusted. "You do," he insisted.

She glanced over her shoulder and momentarily watched the couples. She liked Ian but this, of course, wasn't what she thought of as part of the relationship. She didn't want to lose him. All these thoughts raced through her mind simultaneously. Her cheeks flamed with embarrassment. The sexual intensity was increasing with the other couples.

Then Ian dropped a bomb. He leaned into her ear and whispered, “Do you like your job?”

Hanna was temporarily frozen. She barely understood the threat which seemed unreal in the haze and music.

Her eyes drifted back to the scene as the man with the younger woman stood and took her over to one of the men on the couch and they switched partners giving the younger woman to him. She closed her eyes and complied.

Ian began to unzip Hanna’s skirt in view of the party-goers. Hanna glanced up at him and momentarily gave him a resigned look. He began to push the zipper further down. She reached down, stopped him, and shook her head.

Ian breathed out sharply, his anger evident.

Hanna was oscillating between overly inebriated to embarrassment. She emerged from her stupor, and slurred angrily, “I don’t think I like my job this much.”

She pushed away from Ian, zipped her skirt which was about to fall and buttoned her shirt. She breathed out and walked to the door.

She said, “I can’t believe this,” as she yanked the door open. She took several steps down the hallway then turned back. Ian was holding open the door.

She was about to speak when he stated, “Don’t bother coming to work on Monday.” He was angry and also appeared a bit embarrassed.

She turned away but paused for a few seconds, breathing out. She knew that her great job was probably gone.

Ian held the door open.

Hanna briefly appeared as though she might turn around. For those few seconds, she felt a tinge of regret and did think about turning around and returning to the sex party. She knew that she would have to give herself to all the men in the room before the party ended and maybe some of the women also. She glanced down the hallway at the elevators. Everything that she had worked for was up in smoke. Hanna could feel her shoulders involuntarily begin to turn back to the party though her mind was screaming no. She considered the man on the couch and was repulsed at the thought of him inside her. She shook her head and didn't look back as she stepped towards the elevator.

As the door to the penthouse closed, she could hear Ian laughing.

She walked directly to the elevators.

"Now, what am I going to do?" she said aloud to no one.

In the back of her mind, she could still hear Ian's laugh.

November 9, 2035

Monday

Hanna rose from bed and despite Ian's threat, she got ready for work. The sex party was Saturday night. She hadn't heard from Ian on Sunday.

She showered, made coffee, dressed in her light grey business blazer and skirt, and left for the office. She climbed into her brand-new BMW. It cost her a fortune and took nearly all of her savings. She drove to work and entered the foyer to the Warton Building.

"Good morning, Miss Scott," Frank said cheerfully from the security desk.

"Hi, Frank," Hanna replied to the security officer.

She walked to the elevator and pushed the button that would take her to her office on the fourth floor.

When she arrived, her secretary glanced up at her with concern in her eyes.

Hanna said, "Hi, Peg. What's up?"

"Mister McCaffery is in your office."

"Thanks."

Hanna steeled herself and walked into her office. Ian was sitting on the corner of her desk, glancing at several papers that lay in its center.

"Ian?"

"Ms. Scott."

Hanna kept her expression flat but cocked her head.

McCaffery began, "It's time for your work evaluation."

"I'm guessing that I have some areas of opportunity?"

He smiled grimly. "Actually, our business has turned down a bit because of the economy. I'm sure you understand. So, we need to cut some fat. Your work has been adequate and your record will show that you *were* a good employee."

"Were?"

"Yes, were, opposite of are. I'm afraid that we reluctantly must, at this time, let you go."

"Huh. This doesn't have anything to do with the fact that I wouldn't fuck you and your friends on Saturday night at that party or whatever it was?"

"I have no idea what you're talking about. I am not just letting you go today; several other people are also being released from our employment."

"Why? Wouldn't they fuck your friends, either?"

McCaffery pretended not to hear the comment. He continued, "Companies downsize all the time, Ms. Scott. It's the way of business. This is nothing personal."

"Yeah, the hell it isn't." Tears came to Hanna's eyes. "I thought that we had something, Ian. Why would you want to allow those other men and probably the women there to have my body? That just isn't normal."

"Your severance package is waiting at the security desk. You have ten minutes to clear out your desk here." Ian reached over and pressed an intercom button on the phone that sat on Hanna's desk. "Mrs. Upton, could you send in Frank."

It was obvious that the secretary had been told to call Frank from security once Hanna entered her office.

"Yes, Mister McCaffery."

The door opened and Frank from the security desk walked in and couldn't make eye contact with Hanna.

"Ten minutes, Ms. Scott," McCaffery said, walking out.

Hanna breathed out and said derisively, "Really? Ms. Scott?" She glanced at Frank.

"The guy's been sleeping with me for the last three months. What an asshole."

Frank looked away.

She began placing a few personal things into her briefcase.

Chapter 6

February 26, 2036

Three months later...

An insistent knock came on Hanna Scott's apartment door. She woke groggily, the memory of the fact that she was more than two months behind on her rent, springing to mind. Soon another month would be due.

Her next thought was of her 8th, no 9th unsuccessful job interview that took place yesterday. No one was hiring and her depression was deepening.

"Damn," she whispered aloud.

Her head pounded.

More knocking.

She rose slowly from her couch from the night spent drinking alone. Two bottles of cheap chardonnay sat empty on her coffee table. Did she drink both bottles? She couldn't remember.

More knocking. More insistent.

She glanced at a mirror that hung near her door. Dark circles decorated the space below her eyes. Her hair was a tangled mess. She was barefoot in old sweatpants and her flannel pajama top was half unbuttoned. She glanced down and hastily began buttoning her top wondering how she had fallen so fast into this state. No job... No savings... No prospects...

She couldn't open the door like this with the way she looked.

More insistent knocking.

She held her head which felt like she had been hit with an ax. "Just a minute," she said loudly, then gripped her head again waiting for the pounding to stop.

She finished buttoning her shirt, pushed the tangles out of her hair, walked to the door, and peeked through the peephole.

Her landlord.

"Shit."

He appeared to be annoyed.

She opened the door.

He stood with his arms crossed and an expression of impatience on his face. He was in his forties with a potbelly, a receding hairline, and spoke in some kind of accent, maybe Eastern European. He stepped right inside Hanna's apartment without being invited and glanced at Hanna's misbuttoned shirt that left a gap showing the insides of her breasts.

She noticed, looked down, and crossed her arms over the exposed flesh.

He barked, "You are three months late with your rent. $9000 you owe me. You are going to need to move out."

"No, I'm just two months late." Hanna knew that she had no savings left.

"No, you never pay me for December. Three months and another due soon."

"Look," she said. "I lost my job a few months ago. Can you give me a couple more months to get back on my feet? I can't move out right now. I just had an interview that went really well. I think they're going to higher me," she lied.

"No. You need to be out by end of the week. I have someone interested in this apartment."

"Come on. Maybe we can work something out."

"No, but I'll tell you what, I own another building on the other side of town. The neighborhood is... um... up and coming. The price is twenty-five percent lower. I happen to have two apartments open in that building right now but I think some people are going to take one of them."

Hanna breathed out. "Okay. I'll take a look at it."

"It's furnished, so, if you want to sell some of your furniture, I might be interested in purchasing some of it for your deposit and part of your first month's rent."

Hanna glanced around and nodded. "Can I see the place first?"

The landlord sighed, then said, "I'll meet you there today. One hour. I'm very busy today."

Hanna nodded again.

The landlord turned and walked out, closing the door behind him.

Hanna walked into her kitchen and grabbed two aspirins and washed them down with Coke.

She held her head and stood motionless for several minutes waiting for the aspirin to begin working.

Hanna paused and glanced at her cupboard. She walked to it and pulled open the door and reached for a large bottle of cheap vodka, pouring herself a small glass, and taking a long drink then carried the glass into the bathroom.

She finished the glass, showered, allowing the water to run for several minutes over her still pounding head. She finished showering, dried, wrapped up in her robe, ate an apple, and stood to dress.

Another knock came at her door.

Still in her short robe, she answered.

Her landlord stood there and gave her the once over, his eyes traveling up and down her form, resting on her exposed legs. Her feet were bare.

She pulled the robe tighter around her body.

He said, "This is the address." He handed her a small piece of paper.

She took the paper, quickly glanced at it, and could feel the alcohol beginning to have its effect.

He said, "I need to go over there. You need to meet me in twenty minutes and you can see the place. It's vacant so I won't have to tell the people you are coming. By the way, I have a couple coming to see your apartment tonight at five. Please don't be here."

If looks could kill, the landlord would be lying in a puddle of his own blood.

"Twenty minutes," he said again and he turned and walked away.

Hanna shut the door. She quickly refilled her glass and glanced at the large bottle of vodka. It was nearly empty and she didn't even remotely remember drinking it all. She drank down the clear liquid, setting the glass on her drainboard, then walked to her bathroom.

She dressed, haphazardly put on a bit of makeup, and had another half-glass of vodka. Now feeling no pain, she climbed into her BMW, and drove the twelve blocks to the new apartment. When she arrived, she sighed. This was not a step up. She glanced in her rearview mirror and could see the landlord pull up behind her in a large, black Escalade SUV.

She ate a breath mint then stepped out as a heavy rain soaked the L.A. basin.

He walked to her and gave her a greasy smile. "This way," he said, pointing.

He led her into the lobby of the building and to an elevator. This building was old and the paint showed stains. There was dust in the corners of the brown, tiled floor.

They rode up the elevator in complete silence. Hanna stared forward at the buttons.

The elevator stopped on the fourth floor.

"This way," he repeated as the elevator doors slid open.

He brought her to apartment 414.

She noticed that there was no 413.

He opened the door, and it swung in, then reached in and turned on the light.

Hanna didn't want to enter. She wasn't sure why. She regretted that last drink of Vodka and was feeling quite drunk.

The landlord stepped in first. "Come in. I don't have all day."

She stepped inside.

The apartment wasn't as bad as she had expected. The furnishings were modest but matched, the kitchen, small but clean. The rug had no stains.

He closed the door.

"This way to the bedroom," the landlord said, pointing.

She hesitated for an instant, was it the way he said bedroom? She walked forward.

The bedroom was small and had a queen-sized bed with no bedspread or linen. There was a dresser and a nightstand. A small closet with two sliding, mirrored doors was against a far wall and there was one window that overlooked an alley.

"The bathroom is across the hall."

He ushered her into the bathroom. It had a shower stall, no bathtub, a commode, and a sink with a medicine cabinet.

"I'll take it," Hanna said, with a bit of a slur.

She walked from the bathroom unsteadily and as she neared the front room, the landlord put his hand on her shoulder.

She tightened.

"You still owe me 9,000 back rent."

"But you gave me the impression that you would take my stuff for that." She didn't turn.

"It won't quite cover it and I'll need the back rent before you can move in."

He let his hand drift to her backside.

She didn't move or resist. Was it this or the street?

"Come on. Please don't," she pleaded.

"Maybe I could forgive the back rent?"

She feebly shrugged away.

"Maybe you should move out then."

She stopped and he approached her again. She gave him a resigned look then turned her gaze to the floor. He began unbuttoning her blouse, then slipped his hand inside on her stomach, and began to slide it upward.

She stopped him. "Please no."

He shrugged and backed away. "That same couple that's looking at your place tonight is also going to look at this place tomorrow. It's your choice."

She looked back at the floor.

He walked back to her and finished unbuttoning her blouse.

Again, he smiled.

Her mind went blank.

The next thing she knew, she was bent over the table and he was finishing with his pleasure which took no more than five minutes.

He removed the used condom and fastened his trousers.

She dressed, facing the wall and turning her back to the landlord. She turned back to face him but couldn't make eye contact.

He guiltily watched her dress, but half-smiled, and said, "You can stay here but I will need to occasionally come to visit. Do you understand?"

She nodded.

The next day, the landlord returned with a friend to the apartment that Hanna needed to vacate. Hanna let them in. Again, she had spent the afternoon on her couch, drinking. Two empty bottles of wine sat on her coffee table.

The landlord said, "Good news. The couple loved your apartment and your furniture. They are moving in next week, so you'll need to go. Marty here is going to help you move. He has a truck and some boxes for your stuff. I explained that you don't have money to pay right now, so, he'll accept favors from you."

Hanna didn't expect that. She stood in shock with wide eyes and incredulously said, "No!"

The landlord said, "Take off your clothes Miss. Do it now."

"No!"

Marty stood with a blank expression, glancing from Hanna to the landlord. He wasn't expecting the resistance.

The landlord aggressively walked to Hanna. "I told him that you would pay in your way." He got close to her face. "You and I have an agreement."

She could smell alcohol on his breath.

"He lost money to come here. Take off your clothes."

"No! I'll scream!"

The landlord stepped closer to Hanna. He barked, "We have an agreement!"

She looked away from him and down at the floor.

Two hours later, Hanna lay nude, curled into a ball, and frozen on the couch where they had both used her. She could picture the vivid scene in her mind and her eventual compliance with their demands.

Both had left when Hanna wouldn't respond to them after the rape, it couldn't be called anything else, so the landlord's friend did not help her move. They had both been wearing condoms, so, there would be no DNA evidence. She wouldn't go to the police, anyway. They would ask her embarrassing questions. She couldn't help but feel guilty that this was partly her fault because of *allowing* the landlord the day before. The reality was that it was in no way allowing. It certainly wasn't that; it was shameful coercion. She would pack her few things, get in her car, and drive away, never looking back.

Sometime later, the trunk and back seat of Hanna's BMW were filled. She would leave the furniture. She had no way to take it and no place to store it.

The bleak LA streets were rain-soaked and the wind blew leaves into piles, trapped against the dark grey, wet buildings. Rain pelted her windshield and the street lights reflected off of the wet pavement as she drove away.

Chapter 7

Death Valley, California

March 1, 2036

Phase one of Homeless City was completed with some private fanfare. President Donald Fergusson cut the ceremonial ribbon on an unseasonably hot day, much hotter than any previous spring day on record in Death Valley. The construction crews had been ordered to pause their work for the day and were told to leave the city. Some of the essential city's staff remained and the security team was getting accustomed to the protocols.

Dignitaries in attendance for the ceremony were Governor Roy Blackburn, Attorney General Gilbert Price, Vice President Thomas Gates, and several trusted members of congress. No press and no outsiders were allowed to attend. The fact that this city was for the homeless would remain a secret to the general public for the foreseeable future. All of the construction crews just thought that they were building some kind of specialized futuristic city on the orders of the Governor of California.

The dignitaries gathered at the entrance to the city which would be the initial stop for the homeless as they began their stay. The induction center was the first large building to the right of the boulevard.

Once the ceremony ended, President Fergusson grumbled, "Let's get someplace airconditioned. It's stifling out here." He, like everyone present, was dressed in a dark suit and tie.

Blackburn nodded and ushered the group into the induction center. As they entered the air-conditioned space, Blackburn began speaking, "This is the first stop for the homeless. They will be bathed, strip-searched, medically evaluated, and injected with the identifying and tracking device. Then they will be issued their clothes that will be worn while they reside in the city. All of their clothes will also have tracking devices to help with the laundering and returning to the correct resident. The tracking devices will also allow entry into the underground transportation system and entry into any area that the individual resident has been cleared for. The only traffic allowed on the streets of our city will be security, construction, maintenance, and delivery vehicles."

The induction center was a large warehouse divided in half by an eight-foot wall.

Blackburn said, "The men go this way and the women this." He pointed at signs that directed the men to one side and the women to the other. There were cameras everywhere.

The President glanced around. He asked, "How long until the city is completed?"

Blackburn: "The main parts of the city, most infrastructure, essential services, and security are already completed. The only parts not completed are the residences. That phase is about half-finished. We will expand depending on that need. This city is structured to handle around a million residents, give or take. Once filled, it may be necessary to build another city. Maybe on the other side of the country."

Fergusson shook his head at that assessment. Though the plans were to build another city, it was the last thing he wanted. He glanced around taking in the building and said, "This city is going to cost a fortune to maintain." He appeared disgusted, then finished, "Just to take care of people who are worthless, all losers."

Blackburn said, "Yes, but I think cheaper for the cities in the long run. Having to deal with the homeless was an impossible burden."

Fergusson shook his head and appeared to be reconsidering his decision to go ahead with this project. He said, "I was hoping that this would be a bit more austere."

Blackburn: "In most places, it is. I'll show you one of the residences, the hospital, the center for the drug and alcohol addicted, and the institution for the insane."

Fergusson nodded and shrugged. "I want to see the security building, also."

"Of course," Blackburn replied. He could tell that the President wasn't happy and knew that it reflected on him because Fergusson had relied on him to do the job the way the President wanted it done. The feeling was that this city was just too nice.

Blackburn added, "We have plans to surround the entire city with a fence though we don't think anyone will attempt to walk out. The chances of survival are slim. The Asylum is, of course, securely fenced."

Fergusson nodded again, seemingly bored with the details.

Blackburn said, "This way, please."

He ushered the small group to a wide stairway that would allow twenty people to walk side by side. It led to the subway system. When they reached the bottom of the stairs, they walked onto a well-lit platform with a brightly painted, pale blue subway train awaiting their arrival. Its finish reflected the overhead lights. The train bared a striking resemblance to the Monorail at Disneyland, sleek and modern. It sat behind a floor-to-ceiling glass wall.

Fergusson scratched his head. “Couldn’t we have cut some corners on the costs?”

Blackburn: “Mister President, everything was procured from the list of people that your office provided. I had no leeway to bargain. All of these contractors were not optional as per your instructions.”

Of course, they were all family members and allies of the President. And all had no problem gaffing the government by overcharging. The Vice President glanced away. The Attorney General turned his eyes to the floor. Fergusson reddened a bit then said, “Let’s move on.”

Glass doors between the riders and the trains slid open allowing Fergusson and the group to enter the train. The group stepped through the glass doors and entered the modern subway train’s passenger compartment. Fergusson glanced around. No one sat until he did. He reached over and pushed at the padding on one of the train’s chairs, then sat down in the comfortable seats, again not appearing to be happy, and stared forward.

Blackburn hurriedly spoke into a small device pinned to his suit coat lapel, “You may proceed.”

“Yes, Sir,” a voice could be heard replying.

The train started smoothly and quickly picked up speed.

Fergusson asked, “How fast can this go?”

Blackburn: “Top speed, eighty miles an hour if it’s on the underground expressway. It can only reach around fifty if it’s moving from station to station depending on the distance between.”

Lights outside the moving train blinked as the train passed.

The train stopped at the hospital then moved the group to the Asylum for the clinically insane. Last they inspected the residences. Fergusson was happier after seeing that the apartments where the homeless would reside were just one room, small with a bed that could fold into a couch, a kitchenette, and a bathroom. No TV.

“I’ve seen enough,” Fergusson said after leaving the small apartment.

“But you haven’t seen the security buildings yet.”

Fergusson turned to Vice President Gates and began talking about something that had nothing to do with Homeless City, cutting off Blackburn, and ignoring his response.

Blackburn had the look of a deflated balloon.

“Let’s leave,” Fergusson grumbled.

The group took an elevator down to the subway platform under the resident’s apartments then got back onto the train.

Blackburn spoke into his lapel and said, “Take us back to the garage.”

“Yes, Sir.”

They started off.

Fergusson asked, “Do all of the buildings have train platforms underneath?”

Blackburn, by this time, was a nervous wreck. He quietly said with a slight crack in his voice, "Most buildings have a platform because of the size of some of the complexes. Several platforms do service a group of buildings so in those places, there are well-lit underground walkways to catch the subway to any location within the city. We have a labyrinth of walkways underground mostly used to service the cities utilities. People can, of course, walk to different places outside, but with temperatures reaching 120 degrees in the summer, we don't expect many to do so."

They arrived back at the underground garage where the President's limo was parked.

Blackburn continued to be visibly nervous. This was supposed to be his shining moment before the President. It hadn't worked out that way. The President left no doubt that he wasn't happy with the city.

They walked from the platform to the limo.

Fergusson said, "How long until we begin bringing the homeless here?"

Blackburn responded, "Next week, the first homeless residents will arrive."

Fergusson appeared bored to death, "Take me to the helicopter." He climbed into the back seat of the limo and closed the door leaving Blackburn speechless.

Part 3

The reaping...

Chapter 8

Southern California

April 3, 2036

The roundup of the homeless began quietly, first in Southern California. The idea was to begin slowly to allow some of the bugs in the system to be worked out before the deluge of homeless descended upon the new city in the desert.

Orange County in Southern California was chosen to be the first county where the removal of the homeless would begin. Scores of black vans descended upon the county and began rounding up the homeless first from large encampments that had grown along Interstate 5. As the homeless in the tent and cardboard cities disappeared, everything accumulated in those encampments were scoured away.

The black-clad troops then surrounded all the large homeless encampments around the rest of the county. They swooped in overwhelming numbers to arrest anyone in each encampment. Many resisted and those would be subdued or tasered and forcibly taken out. It was not unusual for some of the homeless to be shot and killed. No stories appeared in any newspaper or on any news station documenting these atrocities. Because the homeless had no advocates in the government, the violations of what minimum rights were left to the American public were ignored.

Within a month, the only homeless left in Orange County were the smattering of individuals who had heard of the removal of the homeless and hid so as not to be abducted. Some homeless who heard the rumors of Homeless City actually volunteered to go.

Phase one of the program was a success. Homeless City was functional, it was staffed with security, professionals, and maintenance crews. The homeless began arriving by the busload and were sorted, evaluated, and separated into the various regions that were most appropriate to their various needs, some to rehab, some to the gated and walled Asylum, and for the homeless who were most functional, to the residential living quarters where they would be given jobs in the community and eventually released.

Now the program would be widened out and the homeless from all over California and then the rest of the country would begin being deported to the desert City.

Chapter 9

Anaheim, California

April 30, 2036

The sun sank on the western horizon and the light dimmed under an overpass near to where Harbor Boulevard crossed the Santa Anna Freeway in Anaheim, California near Disneyland. Graffiti decorated the cement structure with names and vulgarities. Street lights winked on in the distant avenues.

Hanna Scott needed sleep. She sat in the driver's seat of her hybrid van, remembering happier days when she was in college and went to Disneyland with friends for fun. Tonight, this place was deserted but she was not comfortable with where she had parked. She had been driving from place to place for two days and could not find anywhere that felt safe enough to crawl into the back for some nighttime shut-eye, not that there was much room in the back with it being jammed with all her worldly possessions. Just enough space to squeeze herself into a crease. She had grabbed a couple of hours in a Vons grocery store parking lot yesterday but she couldn't stay. If the security guard outside the store saw her asleep in her car, he would, without question, call the police to check her out.

Her van could travel 50 miles without needing to be recharged. Her gas tank was empty. She had traded in her expensive BMW for this hybrid van and had lost a substantial amount of money on the trade but received the van and some cash to live on. There were several recharging stations that allowed you to recharge with no cost to the driver, an old California program that had arisen before the fall of America into tyranny. She had found that those places were the best places to grab a nap during the three hours it took to charge her van. Most of these were located along the highways at rest-stops.

Rumors and urban conspiracy theories were swirling around that people who were homeless were being rounded up and forcibly taken to a city in the desert. Hanna didn't believe these unfounded rumors, though it was true that the homeless had been seen being rounded up and moved. Some rounding up of the homeless had to have been going on for as long as anyone could remember.

Hanna tried to get comfortable in her front seat. She glanced around and could see several men slipping out of the darkness and walking from around a corner, heading towards her van. She had spotted them in her rearview mirror and watched as they approached. Fearful, she quickly started her car and pulled away. The men stared at her as she passed. They appeared to be disappointed.

"Sorry, assholes," she whispered as she drove.

Several times in the last year she had been in situations where she was afraid of being used for sex, most where she had been able to avoid it, and a couple where she had not. Rape, theft, and violence were commonplace among the homeless who could not go to the police for help. The thought of those events still burned red-hot in her memory. She wouldn't allow it to happen again.

She drove for twenty minutes looking for some kind of all-night business where she could park unnoticed.

Hanna thought back to several months ago. Almost overnight, small tent villages began disappearing, the people, tents, and trash, all gone. Is it possible that something was happening to the homeless? Street corners where people had always been seen begging for money were mostly vacant.

She got back on the I5 freeway and drove to a rest-stop that she frequented. As she pulled in, she could see that all of the free charging stations were filled with cars and vans like hers. She pulled into a parking place, used the bathroom, washed her face, brushed her teeth, and then got back into her van, leaned her seat back, made sure her doors were locked, then closed her eyes...

May 1, 2036

Hanna woke to the sound of insistent tapping. It was morning and the Sun was low on the eastern horizon. It shined through the window of her car and made her squint.

A Citizen Guard stood sideways peering into her driver's side window.

Hanna turned to get a better view.

The officer gazed at her with a stern expression and said, “Ma’am?”

Hanna rolled down the window. “Yes?” she responded questioningly.

“Ma’am, could you step out of your car, please?”

“Why? What is this about?”

“Just step out and I’ll tell you.”

Hanna breathed out and opened her door as the cop stepped back. She stood impatiently. She needed a shower and could smell her perspiration. The clothes she was wearing needed to be washed.

“Now, what do you want?” she asked impatiently.

“Ma’am, can I see your license and registration?”

Hanna turned back and got out her driver’s license then handed it to the cop. “I’ve lost my registration,” she lied.

The cop nodded then said, “So, this is your current address?” As he asked, he glanced into her van and could see that the back of it was filled with everything that Hanna owned.

“Yes,” was Hanna’s one-word response.

“Ah-huh. Just a minute. I’ll be back.”

The cop walked back to his patrol car which was parked behind Hanna’s van in a way that made it impossible for her to back out of her parking place. She leaned against her van with her arms folded and waited.

The cop said something into a microphone and waited for a minute then returned to Hanna.

He pulled handcuffs from his belt and said, “Ma’am, I’m going to need to hold you here for a couple of minutes. Could you turn around please?”

“Don’t cuff me, please, I won’t run. I get claustrophobic.”

"Sorry. It's protocol. Turn around please."

He placed the cuffs on Hanna's wrists, ushered her to his patrol car, and slid her into the back seat. He stood outside and gazed into the distance. It appeared that he was looking for or waiting for something.

Two minutes later, an unmarked van and a tow truck pulled into the rest-stop.

The cop had stepped away then returned to Hanna.

She blurted, "You can't hold me! I've done nothing wrong!"

The cop said, "Your registration has expired and you no longer live at this address."

"Okay, so, I know but I'm between homes right now. That was my last address. I'm moving into a new place this week," she lied again.

"Ah-huh."

Two men dressed in dark suits stepped up and one said, "We'll take it from here."

The cop nodded and pulled Hanna from the squad car.

The two men walked Hanna to the unmarked van.

"Stop it! Where are you taking me?"

"You are being detained and relocated, Ms. Scott. We have a new program for the homeless that is not optional. You are going to be taken there now."

He took her by the arm and turned her to face the dark van. "Spread your legs. Are you carrying any weapons?"

She shook her head.

He quickly patted her down then said, "Get in the van, please."

She didn't move.

The police car pulled away leaving Hanna with the two men. The tow truck began hooking-up to Hanna's van. She was having trouble processing how fast this had happened to her. Her van had been hoisted and the tow truck started away.

The mysterious men in dark suits pushed Hanna unceremoniously into the back of their large van. No one else was inside. There were no windows and two benches that lined each side of the van with D-rings on the floor and on the front edge of the benches.

The second suited man then frisked Hanna, again. This time more thoroughly, checking her pockets and every place where she could hide anything.

She began to fear another sexual assault, but he was all business. He undid her cuffs and sat her down with a D-ring between her legs, then cuffed her hands to the ring on the bench.

Nothing else was said. The doors to the back of the van were closed. It pulled away from the rest-stop and onto the freeway, picking up speed.

Hanna dozed as the miles passed. She hadn't slept much in the last few days and she was depleted...

She woke, startled, sensing that the van was slowing, switching directions, and driving over speed bumps. She thought that she would be taken to the police station and wasn't sure how long she had slept.

The back doors opened and bright white light filled the back of the van. One of the men in the suits stepped inside with Hanna and unhooked the handcuffs. He didn't replace the cuffs and allowed Hanna to step off the van without restraints.

To Hanna's surprise, she stepped into a large bustling warehouse. There were lines of homeless men and women being processed, most in dirty and tattered clothes. The men were on one side of the warehouse and the women on the other. There were more men than women but not many more.

She looked around and seeing no posted signs, could not figure out where she was. Nothing here was marked. Men and women dressed in black jumpsuits with no sleeve markings directed the homeless people and kept them in their lines. Heavily armed Citizen Guards with armbands and bad attitudes, also in the same jumpsuits, stood at the entrances and in various places around the warehouse. Some patrolled.

Hanna gazed around disoriented, not quite able to comprehend fully what she was witnessing. A male guard pushed her into the line with the women.

She stood there for a minute then whispered to a woman standing in front of her, "Where are we?"

The woman obviously did not want to respond. She leaned back slightly and said, "Don't know. They picked me up and brought me here. That's all I know."

A male guard monitoring the line shouted, "Shut up in line."

The woman distanced herself from Hanna.

The guard tried to stare a hole through Hanna but she stared back at him defiantly.

He walked over but she didn't blink.

"Am I going to have trouble with you, lady?"

"Not if you get out of my face."

He glanced around then grabbed her by her shirt and brought her face close to his. "We can do this the hard way if you want."

Hanna snapped, "Who the fuck are you people? Am I under arrest? Am I going to prison?"

He smiled grimly in warning then released her roughly and glanced at the other homeless around. They all shrank back. Hanna got the feeling that they might have witnessed things that Hanna had not. She quieted.

The guard said nothing and walked away.

The line moved quickly. Vans with more homeless like Hanna arrived delivering additional people to this facility which made the line behind her grow.

One of the homeless men, who was probably not mentally well, became unruly in line and two guards approached and tasered him. He fell in a quivering heap and they took him away on a stretcher.

Hanna reached the front of the line. She asked the woman processing her, “Where am I?”

“You are being relocated.”

“Relocated? To where?”

The woman shrugged.

Hanna stared at her, bewildered.

The woman motioned Hanna with her hand and said, “Proceed forward, please.”

Hanna did as she was asked.

She entered a large room with rows of locker room-type benches all fixed to the floor. Once the benches were filled with around twenty women, another black jump-suited woman with a bad attitude stepped up to a microphone at a small podium in front of the benches.

She pointed then said, “When I instruct you, you will step through those doors. A bus will take you to your new home.”

One woman raised her hand to ask a question.

The woman at the podium barked, “Did I say, any questions?” She nodded to two black jump-suited women who opened the doors. All the women on the benches stood, turned, and walked through.

Another woman waited as the homeless women filled the room. She commanded, "Line up."

The women all glanced around uncomfortably.

Hanna thought back to some of the stories out of Nazi Germany and the relocation of the German Jews. She stood with her arms wrapped over her chest and became more afraid.

After a few minutes, two doors opened on the other side of the room. A different black-clad woman stepped in and said, "This way. Move it."

Hanna thought of how this entire experience was dehumanizing.

Once all of Hanna's group were in the room, a different black-clad woman came in and said, "Follow me."

Everyone stood and followed the woman. No one protested. She led them through a long hallway and into a separate room with more homeless women. There were at least eighty waiting in this room. Two roll-up doors ground open and several black-clad women stood in front of the doors. One stepped forward and said, "Line up. Two straight lines in front of each door."

The women quietly lined up.

The woman continued to give commands, "We have two buses. Enter and walk to the back, filling each seat. We have just enough seats to transport you to your destination."

One woman in the middle of one of the lines shouted, "What destination?!"

The woman who was giving instructions glanced at the woman who asked the question and gave her a disgusted look. Then she continued her instructions, "Start loading the buses."

Two guards asked each woman if they were carrying any weapons or anything that could be used as a weapon. After the women's response, they frisked each at the front of each line just before they entered the bus.

They reached Hanna, frisked her, and nodded for her to enter the bus. Once on the bus, Hanna found a seat. One of the homeless women would not let anyone sit by her leaving the last woman who entered, standing with no other place to sit.

The woman who had been giving the instructions walked onto the bus. She asked the woman not allowing the last woman to sit, "Is there a problem?"

It was obvious that the lady who would not allow anyone to sit by her was not mentally right. She snapped, "I don't like people sitting by me. I don't like people."

The woman giving the instructions touched her ear and said, "I got a 10 in here."

She glanced at the obstinate woman and said, "Oh. You don't like people sitting by you? Well, that makes sense." The sarcasm was obvious.

Two huge, black-clad men walked onto the bus, stepped over to the obstinate woman, and without a word, tasered her. She dropped like quivering Jell-O and they unceremoniously dragged her roughly off the bus.

The woman giving instruction turned to the wide-eyed woman who didn't have a seat and said, "Sit."

The woman quickly did as she was instructed.

The black-clad woman then walked off the bus. The driver closed the doors, started the bus, and pulled out. There were no windows and the driver pulled closed a partition in the front of the bus that prevented anyone from seeing out of the windshield. Dim lights lit the interior and the smell of unwashed bodies drifted throughout.

This was like a ride into a nightmare, Hanna thought.

Chapter 10

Death Valley, California

May 1, 2036

The bus slowed and proceeded over several speed bumps. Sleeping deeply, Hanna was jarred left then right. She bumped the lady sitting next to her and the lady roughly pushed Hanna away.

"Watch it!" the lady barked.

"Oh, sorry," Hanna responded. She had been sleeping so soundly that she hadn't felt the bus slow.

The woman said, "Bitch."

Hanna didn't respond. She glanced towards the front of the bus. As it slowed to a stop, the partition slid open and a woman dressed in a black jumpsuit stepped into the front in view of the riders. She was tall and stocky and like everyone Hanna had encountered since her abduction, sporting a bad attitude.

"Your attention."

The woman waited until the bus quieted and all eyes were on her. She breathed out as if her needing to make an announcement was an unacceptable imposition. She began, "Congratulations, you have reached your destination. This place is somewhere you will get the chance to get your lives back together.

This isn't a prison. It's just a short stop on your way back into society."

One of the women seated blurted, "How do I get out of here?"

The black-clad woman glared at the woman who spoke then said, "All of your questions will be answered, even the dumb ones."

The rebuked woman didn't respond. Low chuckles broke out on the bus.

The black-clad woman continued, "Upon exiting the bus, you will follow the directions of our attendants. You will shower and be given new clothes, then checked for lice. If lice are found, your head will be shaved. Now exit the bus after me."

Hanna stood with the rest of the homeless and exited into a scorching day. Though the bus was parked under a structure and in the shade, the air was stifling. Damn hot for May. At least eight armed guards were standing outside this unloading zone as if the homeless might try to run.

Hanna thought as she observed the guards, run? Where would we run to? She glanced around at the desert landscape. Geez, she thought again. The middle of nowhere. From this position, it was impossible to see the rest of the city.

They proceeded into a large warehouse-like building. It had high ceilings with exposed beams and windows lining the highest parts of the dull blue walls. There were cameras everywhere in the beams and lights hung down and lit the warehouse brightly. The floor was smooth, grey cement. Two signs greeted the bus riders. It pointed the women left and the men right, separated by an eight-foot dull blue wall that didn't extend to the ceiling.

Hanna glanced again at the cameras.

The head woman who had spoken to the bus riders stepped aside as the women from the bus entered a large room with what appeared to be rows of benches fixed to the floor. The women sat.

The head woman walked to a podium and said, "Your attention, again."

All eyes turned to her.

She began to speak, "Here, you will be issued clothing with built-in electronic devices that will have your information contained within, where you will be housed, where you work, and other information to help with laundering and tracking. Remove all of your clothes and proceed to the showers. If you need to use the bathroom facilities they are located to your left against the far wall. Move it, ladies, we have another bus arriving in ten minutes and we need you out of here. Place your old clothes into these hampers. Your new clothes will be issued after your examination."

There were a dozen clothes hampers on wheeled dollies, all half-filled with the typical clothing of the homeless, tattered and soiled.

Hanna glanced back up at the cameras. Most of the other women began to undress. A few went into the bathroom.

The black-clad, headwoman barked again. "When you have undressed, line up on me, here."

As the nude women began to line up, several jump-suited women wearing gloves walked the line looking for lice. They pulled several women out of the line, then took them into a separate room. The women in line watched as they walked away, then a different group of jump-suited women stepped up to the line, and began cutting the remaining women's hair just above their shoulders. A couple resisted. They were tasered and dragged away. No questions and no debate. They hit the ground quivering.

Once the women's hair was cut, the headwoman said, "You go shower. You go shower. You go shower," one by one until what was left of the first twenty women were in the showers.

Hanna undressed and had needed to use the restroom so she was in the second group. She proceeded to the line and stood with her arms crossed over her breasts as did most of the women waiting.

Once the first group finished, Hanna and the second group received their hair cut, then were directed into the steamy open shower room.

The head woman again exhorted the showering women to hurry.

As they finished and each woman walked from the showers, they were instructed to step into some kind of anti-fungus solution for their feet, then pointed through another door. They were not given towels and they dripped where they stood. Several of the women who had been pulled from the line rejoined the others back in the showers. Their hair was cut short, no more than a quarter-inch long but every other woman's hair was also cut above their shoulders.

There arose some protest and grumbling at the women's treatment, but the attending, black-clad women were strict and aggressive and though some of the naked homeless women were aggressive also, the black-clad women took no crap. Several of the homeless women were tasered and dragged naked across the wet floor and unceremoniously dropped into a corner where they were handcuffed to floor D-rings.

It was frightening and far worse than any treatment that these women might have experienced in any prison. It was obvious that the term civil rights had no place or power in this homeless institution if it had any remaining power in the United States at all.

As the tasered women woke, they couldn't stand or sit because of the constriction of the restraints. They had to lay or half-lay unclothed and wait until someone would pay attention to them. A couple became unruly and loud but the black-clad women walked over, tasered them again, and just walked away. There was not ever an attempt to reason. What you got was predictable and administered with no apparent concern.

With goosebumps, more from fear than cold, Hanna walked in the procession of homeless women into another room with no chairs and six doors, each door with an attendant standing outside. The women stood and waited.

After a few minutes, the attendants began ushering the homeless women, one by one, into an examination room.

It was Hanna's turn. When she entered, the attendant exited and some kind of female medical professional in a white coat said, "On the table, please." The woman was all business. She snapped on rubber gloves.

Hanna laid on the examination table.

The woman began a thorough exam, pushing at Hanna's stomach, examining her breasts, checking ears, eyes, nose, mouth, throat, temperature, a pelvic, then last a cavity search.

Hanna was silent for several minutes as the doctor did her work. Hanna finally said, "What is this place and why is everyone here so mean?"

The doctor glanced up at a camera on the corner of the ceiling then reluctantly said, "What's your name?"

"Hanna."

"This place, Hanna, is about to process nearly a million homeless. Many of whom are not okay. The strictness is mostly to get everyone to their proper placement. Stand up for me so I can get a look at your spine and posture."

Hanna stood and turned to face the wall.

The doctor continued to talk. She gripped Hanna's hips and turned her slightly as she looked her over. "I know you're spooked by this whole thing. I've been told that though life here will be austere, it won't be abusive. I was a bit taken aback when I saw some of the treatment also."

Hanna nodded.

"Any back pain, Hanna?"

"No."

"HIV, Hepatitis?"

"No, but I've been raped a couple of times in the last few months."

"I'm sorry, Hanna. I've heard that story a lot. We'll get you tested."

"Thanks."

"You look good, Hanna. Very healthy. You have beautiful skin. How long were you homeless?"

"Three, maybe four months."

"You're in a lot better shape than most of the people coming in here. One last thing. Please sit back on the examination table."

The doctor took out a syringe with a long, thick needle and then swabbed Hanna's upper arm with alcohol.

Hanna glanced at the needle. It looked as though it would hurt upon entry.

The doctor sprayed an analgesic onto the site to help deaden the pain and then pushed the needle into Hanna's arm.

Hanna asked, "What is this?" She winced.

"It's a tracking and identifying device. It will keep track of you while you're here. It's for everything from food and toiletries, to clothes, to housing, to work."

A trickle of blood ran down Hanna's arm. The doctor cleaned it, then placed a bandage on the small wound with some antibacterial cream.

"That's it, Hanna. All done."

The doctor then pushed a button. An attendant walked in from a door on the opposite side of the examination room.

"She's going to take you to get some clothes."

"Thanks. I would appreciate that."

"I bet," the Doctor commented, nodding. She suddenly looked tired.

The attendant abruptly said, "Let's go."

The attendant walked Hanna to another line with women all having a bandage on their right upper arms.

Hanna was then ushered into a large room with black-clad women sitting at tables around the room. Each table had stacks of clothes and shoes behind the sitting attendant. When a table opened up, Hanna was taken to it.

The attendant said, "Full name?"

"Hanna Scott."

The woman typed on a keyboard then scanned Hanna's arm with some kind of handheld device. It beeped. "How tall are you?"

"5 3."

The woman grabbed three small jumpsuits and scanned the barcodes. She grabbed three plastic bags, each containing underwear, and scanned the bar codes on each.

"Shoe size?"

"6."

The attendant grabbed one pair of flip-flops and 2 pairs of shoes and scanned a barcode on the back of each and then three pairs of socks scanning each. She stacked the clothes then handed the stack to Hanna and said, "Next."

Hanna was then walked to a chair where she could get dressed. By this time, she had been naked for over two hours. This whole process was again, dehumanizing.

Happy to finally be dressed, Hanna walked with the attendant into another room where now fully dress women, some who had been on her bus and others that she didn't recognize, sat in rows before a small portable podium. All now had shorter hair, a few with their hair buzz-cut. No one smiled.

The head lady from the bus walked to the podium and tapped the mic. "Your attention. Your assimilation into our little town will be complete when you are taken to your places of residents. Then you will be given jobs. These will not be optional. We will assess you, as we collect information about you, then you will be placed. Anyone who displays antisocial tendencies will be confined in our institution for the mentally and criminally insane. There you will probably spend the rest of your life. It's a place to be avoided. Once you get to your residence, you will, within a couple of hours, be met by a social worker who will explain further the rules and regulations of our community which will include how and when you might be released back into society. We have a bagged lunch for you when you reach your residence. Now, line up at the bus and we will transport you to your residence."

Everyone stood. Hanna glanced around at her surroundings that now seemed more like a frustrating dream than it did the reality that she now found herself in. It was now much easier to get a look at the women who accompanied her than it was when they were not dressed. It seemed more appropriate to look directly at each. It was a cross-section of society, a melting pot in the same way the L.A. basin was a melting pot. There were African Americans, Hispanics, Asians, Caucasians, and other ethnicities in what appeared to be nearly equal numbers. The ages varied from late teens to late seventies. Most of the women looked like life had been hard.

Hanna walked to the forming line and a young woman who lined up behind her softly said, "Hi."

Hanna turned.

The young woman whispered, "Can I sit with you on the bus?"

"Okay?"

"Good, thanks," the young woman quietly replied, then, "I'm so afraid. I... um... Thanks." Deciding not to say more, she leaned away from Hanna and took a deep breath.

The line began to move and the women stepped towards the bus. Once on, Hanna looked for a place with two open seats. She sat and the young woman slid in next to her. The bus continued to fill as the young woman sat with her hands in her lap and her head down.

Once everyone was seated, the bus started forward out of the garage.

Hanna turned to the woman and said, "I'm Hanna."

"Hi, Hanna, I'm Trish, short for Patricia. Thanks again."

Trish was no more than twenty, maybe younger with dirty blond hair, soft brown eyes, and pale, freckly skin. She appeared as though she hadn't had much food to eat lately. She was painfully thin. Hanna remembered seeing her naked in the line. She had prominent ribs, thin arms and legs, and boney shoulders. The bones in her face were too prominent.

"No problem, Trish."

Trish said shakily, "Where have we landed ourselves. This seems like some kind of waking nightmare."

"I know. I was just thinking the same thing."

"My arm hurts," Trish said, rubbing the site of the injection where the security device was implanted.

"Mine is a bit sore also."

They both stared forward as the bus left the garage and pulled onto the city's main boulevard.

This bus had large windows and they had a view of the city that showed the wide boulevard, completely clean with no cars but several service vehicles were parked and others moved up and down the street. No people walked anywhere. There were tall towers with cameras pointing in all directions and no visible buildings over one story, except for one, a tall building that was marked security in big black letters on a sign above the double doors to enter the building. On the roof of the security building were several satellite dishes and tall antennas of some kind. Camera towers were also visible there.

The bus continued down the main boulevard then pulled onto a side street and into a garage that led underground.

When the bus stopped, the driver told the women to exit.

Hanna stood with the rest of the people on the bus. Trish didn't stand.

"Let's go, Trish," Hanna said.

"Can we wait for everyone else to get off?"

"Okay?"

"I... um..." she stopped.

"We can wait," Hanna said quietly.

"Thanks," Trish said, staring down into her lap.

"What's up with you, Trish?"

"Some of the women were mean to me. They scared me when we were in the showers. They said things to me. I don't want to see them."

Hanna began to think that Trish had more going on than she originally thought.

"What did they say?"

Trish looked around then back at her folded hands. "Something about using me. Things that they were going to make me do."

Hanna's eyes widened. She responded, "Oh, geez. Okay, Trish. I think we're going to find out where our rooms are. That should be a relief."

"Yeah, I guess."

Once all the women passed, Trish and Hanna got up and walked from the bus.

There, the forty women gathered around another black jump-suited woman who began to speak. "Attention. I am going to get you to your rooms. You are under housing unit 1B200. This unit holds 1000 women. You will each get a private room. The cafeteria that services this unit and the men's unit is in the adjacent building. I will give you your room numbers on a piece of paper. A social worker will meet you in your rooms sometime in the next 2 to 3 hours. Do not leave your room until you have met with the social worker. After, you can wander around a bit. Each room has a sink and commode but no shower. In your room, you will receive a bagged lunch and a folder with a map of this housing complex, and one of the entire city, including the underground rail system that will take you to and from your jobs. Come up when I call your names and I will point you to the elevator that will take you to your room."

The woman paused and got out a clipboard and began calling names in alphabetical order. The As, Bs, Cs, and on until, "Patricia Richards."

That's me," Trish said. She walked up and was handed a piece of paper with her name and a room number.

"Elevator B," the woman said, pointing.

Trish glanced around. She lingered for a moment then began to walk to the elevator then stopped when she heard. "Hanna Scott."

She watched Hanna get the paper with the room number.

"Elevator B."

Hanna nodded and turned to the elevator. She could see Trish waiting. Hanna walked up.

"What's your room number, Trish?"

“1B2023.”

Hanna glanced at her piece of paper, “I’m in 1B2026.”

“Good,” Trish said. “Maybe we’re close.”

“Yep,” Hanna agreed.

They walked to the elevator then pushed the up button. The elevator opened onto a hallway that seemed to go on forever. It was dimly lit with dark grey indoor and outdoor carpet and light grey walls. On the ceilings were lights and cameras about every twenty feet.

They glanced at a room by the elevator, 1B2020. Then started down the hall and quickly reached Trish’s room.

“This is me,” Trish said.

Hanna’s room was across the hall and down a door.

“I’m here,” Hanna said with a nod, then “We’re close.”

“That’s good,” Trish said apprehensively.

“Okay, well, I’ll talk to you later.”

“Okay.”

Hanna reached for her doorknob. The door spoke in a female disembodied robotic voice, “Hanna Scott.” The door lock clicked and Hanna turned the knob and walked into her austere new home.

She heard another voice say, “Patricia Richards.” The door clicked.

Hanna stood and looked around. She saw one small bed that looked like it folded in to be a couch, a small kitchenette with a counter, and one chair. Next to the bed was one side table and a large clock on one wall. The rest of the walls were bare with the exception of two cameras in the corners of the ceiling. Hanna walked and opened one of two doors which opened into a bathroom. There were two cameras in the ceiling, a toilet, a small sink, and no shower. She opened the second door, a closet with three hangers and another camera in the center of the ceiling. There was one dresser on the wall by the door.

Hanna walked over and lifted the lunch then sat on the chair, looked around, stared at one of the cameras, breathed out, and sighed, “Geez.”

Chapter 11

Washington DC

The Oval Office

The homeless streamed by bus into Homeless City. On the east coast, a new Homeless City had broken ground as the first hundred thousand people from California deported into the city had only emptied a small portion of the southern part of the state.

In the Oval Office, President Donald Fergusson sat behind his desk with his Vice President, Thomas Gates, and his Chief of Staff, Adam Cruz, standing before him. Both men stood silently as the President focused his displeasure on them.

"How am I going to get out of this Homeless City debacle?"

Gates said, "I talked to Roy. He said that he's pretty happy with how cleaned up Southern California is becoming. The only problem that he mentioned, the last time I talked to him, was that the Asylum in Homeless City was filling up faster than he expected. They have been placing anyone who's unruly there not just the plain crazy. I think that when we build the east coast version, we should make the Asylum portion much larger."

Fergusson snapped, "We can't afford the East Coast version! That's the point."

Cruz said, "But they've already broken ground."

Fergusson barked, "Stop them. I don't want another dime spent on this program."

Cruz seemed to visibly shrink. "Um, okay. We can do that."

"Do it," Fergusson said abruptly.

Cruz and Wilson both glanced at each other, then nodded.

"Blackburn," Fergusson said in disgust. "I never should have appointed him to take charge of this program. This is his fault. We need to come up with some other kind of solution for this homeless problem. Something more permanent."

"I don't understand?" Cruz said questioningly.

"I need to talk to Atwood Colter privately."

Cruz said, "I will contact him immediately."

"Do it now. He needs to come here," Fergusson continued now with his agitation growing.

"Yes, Sir, Mister President."

"Both of you go. I need to think. I want to know when he will arrive."

Cruz said, "Yes, Sir."

They both walked downcast from the room. As they entered the outer office, they glanced at each other with the same thought, Fergusson was becoming increasingly unstable and erratic.

Chapter 12

Death Valley, California

Homeless City

One week in, the first day on the job.

Hanna made her way to the shower room to get ready for work. As she entered, she marveled that this was the largest shower room that she had ever seen. Rows of lockers stood in a warehouse-sized facility, no less than two hundred showerheads protruded from the walls and from freestanding towers that appeared like trees in a vast yellow tiled forest. One side of the shower room was not visible from the other because of steam and mist that filled the air.

Upon entry to and exit from the shower room, each person's towel and change of clothes were scanned to prevent theft. Hanna had seen several women stopped for not having their proper towels. The women were taken away by the Citizen Guard.

Hanna took off her clothes and slipped on her flip-flops. She glanced around and a few benches over could see Trish disrobe and step towards the showers. She hadn't seen Trish since the first day. Trish was just skin and bone with protruding ribs and hip bones. She appeared emaciated. Hanna thought for sure that

Trish was going to follow her around like a puppy, but Trish had not.

Hanna walked up. "Hi, Trish."

"Oh, Hanna," Trish said, turning around. "Um, hi."

She appeared as though she wanted to find something to cover herself with and crossed her arms over her chest.

Hanna said, "I haven't seen you since we got here."

"No, well, I was sick and they brought me to the infirmary. I hadn't been eating and I had some electrolyte problems. I was dehydrated. I guess my heart was skipping around. They put me in bed for a few days and on an IV. I feel a lot better now."

"That's great."

"Yeah, well, I got to shower. I start my new job today."

"Where are you working?"

"At the Eastern Library. I actually was a librarian before I became homeless."

"I'm working there, too."

"You are?"

"Yep. They gave me a choice of the kitchen or the library. No work here for an advertising executive. The choice was a no-brainer."

"That's what you did before, um, well, you became homeless?"

"Yep. Let's shower."

It seemed that Trish wanted to ask more questions about Hanna's becoming homeless, but she refrained. Trish paused then said meekly, "Okay." She turned for the showers.

Hanna followed her and walked to the nearest open shower head. They both washed quickly.

Afterward, they picked up their towels and as they dried, Hanna said, "I can't believe that we are working together. That's great. Since you were a librarian, you can show me the ropes."

"Ah-huh," Trish responded in her usual reserved manner and dressed quickly, barely dry.

"Hey, Trish, I think everything's going to be okay," Hanna said, trying to be somewhat reassuring, though, she didn't feel that way herself. Everything in this odd city, so far, was disturbing.

"Maybe."

"Maybe we can both get out of here pretty soon."

"I guess."

"What's wrong?"

"I don't really have anything to go to out there in the world. I don't like change," Trish responded while Hanna slipped on the state-issued, ill-fitting bra and panties, stepped into the grey jumpsuit, and zipped up the front.

Trish continued, "I don't want to stay and I don't want to go."

"Maybe we can get out together and help look after each other until we get back on our feet."

"Yeah, maybe."

"Let's go get breakfast."

"Okay."

They finished dressing, left the shower room, and walked down the wide steps to the train platform where black-clad employees of the city stood amidst the residents.

Hanna was surprised at how many people there were waiting for the trains. The city was filling up. All the residents were dressed exactly the same in grey jumpsuits. All had the same haircut except for a smattering of residents both male and female with shaved heads. All the employees were also dressed the same in black jumpsuits and some had tasers strapped to their sides the way sheriffs of the old west wore their sidearms. Occasionally, Citizen Guards appeared in their black and dark green camo with red armbands sporting the letters CG. Some were in helmets, carrying automatic military weapons, and were catching the trains with the many residents that waited. Most of the employees of the city would not wait in line but would push their way to the front and would enter before the residents.

Trish glanced over her shoulder constantly as if she expected to be apprehended at any moment. Hanna watched her with growing concern.

The train service was impressive with trains arriving one after another and filling with riders.

Hanna and Trish boarded and sat together on comfortable seats as the train left for the cafeteria. Hanna glanced over at Trish and half-smiled. Trish appeared as if she had just been informed that she had terminal cancer.

"It's going to be okay, Trish. You'll see," Hanna said, reaching for her hand, gripping it, and giving it a squeeze.

Trish nodded and held Hanna's hand tightly.

The light in the moving train was low and long vertical, dim, yellow lights in the tunnel could be seen through the windows flashing by as the underground train picked up speed.

Chapter 13

Death Valley, California

Vincent Ravello was the foreman on the construction crew whose job it was to extend the last phase of Homeless City's residential apartment buildings outward toward the northwest of the current city.

Three days ago, he got the word from Governor Roy Blackburn, "Get this job finished. The city is about to fill up."

Everyone had seen the lines of busloads of homeless streaming into the city.

No one wanted the job done more than Ravello. Death Valley would soon reach temperatures of more than 100 degrees during the day, and by summer, you would need EVA suits provided by NASA to endure the heat to come. He didn't want to spend another summer there.

As it was, the early morning was already hot in the low 80s and the wind mild. Choking dust rose in billows throughout the construction zone.

Jose Garza worked one of the backhoes digging out the dried lakebed for the underground portion of this phase of this residential complex. At about fifteen feet, he struck cement, fracturing an underground slab. It cracked and a crevasse opened wide into what appeared to be an underground chamber. He climbed out of his rig and peered at the wide crack. The smell was musty like wet rug mixed with dried mushrooms.

"Hey boss," he called, seeing Ravello standing above the excavation.

"What is it, Garza?"

"I think we got a problem."

Ravello walked around the ridge of the excavation and down the earthen ramp that led to the backhoe. Garza was staring at the fractured underground structure.

"What's up?"

"There's been some kind of building down here."

Ravello pulled a blueprint that had been rolled up in his back pocket. He unrolled it, flipped through the several pages, studied it, and said, "There isn't anything showing on the blueprints this far away from the base."

The abandoned Air Force base was north of Homeless City and though underground structures were identified in the blueprints, none extended out to this distance away from the base.

Ravello stepped into the hole and glanced at the broken cement. He peered down through the crack that was widening as the fractured cement fell into the hole.

"Does anyone have a flashlight?"

"I got one," Garza said.

He climbed back up into his cab then back down and handed the light to Ravello who bent and shined it into what appeared to be an empty room. The walls were oddly molded and discolored. The mold appeared as splashes on the walls and floor as though something liquid had been haphazardly flung in all directions causing the mold to grow.

There wasn't anything else in the room and the door in the underground space appeared to be sealed as if it was a door to an underground vault.

Ravello rose and said, "I don't think this is any big deal. I don't want to stop progress because of an old abandoned empty room."

Garza wasn't so sure, though, and he said, "Maybe you should check with someone."

"Nah. Go through it. We need to keep on schedule."

Garza shrugged and nodded. He climbed back into the backhoe's cab and began pulling out large pieces of mold-covered cement.

Ravello watched from the top of the hole. By the time Garza got to the bottom of the large underground room, it was obvious that it had been abandoned, was completely empty, and cleaned of whatever it had been used for. The only thing noticeable was the odd mold that covered most of the surfaces of the broken-up cement. The mold was black with a green tinge. It shimmered in the sunlight and seemed to dry instantly as the sun hit it. A light powder rose from the odd mold into the air and drifted in the breeze towards Homeless City.

Bulldozers began scraping large piles of dirt and the remnants of the room into trucks to be carried off and used for landfills near Long Beach and a construction project near the coast close to the border with Mexico. The breeze picked up and blew dust from the hole over the workers. Ravello squinted as some of the dust struck him in the eye. There was a slight burning sensation and he turned from the excavated hole and coughed, then got some distance and was glad to not have to slow progress and catch hell from Blackburn.

Chapter 14

Homeless City

After breakfast, Hanna and Trish reported to the Eastern Library at 7:30 am. The library was supposed to open for the first time at 9:00 am. There would be just enough time for some training. A small group of ten women and five men waited outside the front double doors. No one spoke.

A black-clad woman stepped out of the doors and said, “My name is Ann Voss. I’m the head librarian. Please enter the building.”

They walked in as a group. The library was a large but mostly empty room. It seemed that there were more books to come. There were a dozen rows of shelves on one side labeled fiction and half a dozen rows on the other side marked nonfiction.

Voss continued when everyone was in the doors and she had their attention, “I will begin your training on the computer system and filing of the books. We have a limited supply for now but more books are on the way. We will not have other media that people are used to finding at their local library, books only, but it will be sufficient for our residents who will not have access to TV, movies, computers, radio, or audiobooks. It will have to do. You will each have 12-

hour shifts and, after today, will work from 9:00 am to 9:00 pm. Now proceed to the checkout desk."

For the next hour and a half, the fifteen people received training on the checkout procedures taking turns working the computers, practicing re-shelving the books, and bringing up books to be checked out.

By 9:00, several people had lined up at the doors. The doors were opened and the people entered and wandered the library, perusing the bookshelves for books to check out.

Both Hanna and Trish worked at the checkout desk and a steady stream of people came and went. There was a two-book limit and each person had their arm scanned, where the device had been injected, to attach the book to them.

By 7:00 pm, both Hanna and Trish were becoming tired. This had been a full day with two more hours to go. The residents of the city had trickled in all day with no large rush but the people entering had been steady.

Hanna turned to Trish, and said, "Trish, I'm going to take my last break. I'm beat. I'll be back in ten minutes. I hope there's a little coffee left."

Trish nodded.

Hanna walked into the breakroom and to the coffee that had been provided for the workers. She poured a small cup, kicked off her shoes, and put her feet up on an adjacent chair. The breakroom was small, painted pale yellow, and had a table surrounded by a dozen plastic chairs.

She gazed around and thought, how in the hell did I end up here? She shook her head. Once she had finished her coffee, she used the restroom, and walked back to the checkout desk to relieve someone else for their last break.

A man was standing by the checkout desk and Trish was checking out his two books. He looked familiar from behind. What was it? The way he stood, his posture, his hair, the shape of his head? It was something.

Hanna walked behind the counter and looked more closely at the man. He had a short beard. His hair was brown with just the slightest hint of red as if he was probably a redhead as a child. Hanna's eyes widened.

"Jack?"

The man glanced up. Was that a hint of recognition? He quickly hid it.

"Jack Morgan?"

"No, I'm sorry. You have mistaken me for someone." He turned to Trish. "Are we finished?"

"Yes," she said, not quite knowing how to handle the awkward situation.

The man took his books and quickly walked out of the double doors.

Hanna walked over to Trish. What was that guy's name?"

"John Black."

"Huh," Hanna said, somewhat mystified.

"What is it, Hanna? How much did he look like the guy you mentioned?"

"Like an identical twin," Hanna said as she walked to relieve a librarian near Trish for his last break.

Trish said, "I hear that everyone has someone out in the world who looks nearly exactly like themselves."

"Yeah, I guess," Hanna responded. Then, "Huh?"

They finished their shifts and took the trains back to their residential units. Hanna could not take her mind off of the man that she had seen at the library. Jack didn't have a beard back when she knew him. It had been at least two, no maybe three years, before. They had been in a torrid relationship, short and intense. When Jack said he had to leave, it was devastating. As the time passed, Hanna began to lose the image of the man in the library. She had only seen him for a minute. Maybe it wasn't the Jack she knew... She thought, too weird.

Chapter 15

Washington DC

The Oval Office

President Fergusson sat behind his desk in the Oval Office stewing. He could feel his blood pressure rising by the second. This homeless situation was becoming ridiculous. The ground that had already been broken in South Carolina for the next Homeless City had been stopped but now congress had a new proposal for Texas to be the next location. The governors and congressmen liked the way the first Homeless City had cleaned up several states.

Fergusson glanced at his clock, 10:35 am. Atwood Colter was five minutes late. Just as that thought entered the President's mind, there was a knock at his door.

"Come in."

His secretary walked into the room and announced, "Mister Colter here to see you."

"Send him in."

Atwood Colter entered the Oval Office closing the door behind him. He was tall and painfully thin with a short grey beard and a full head of grey hair. He wore wirerimmed glasses and was the appointed head of the Citizen Guard's Secret Service. This group of specialized law enforcement had, in the last two years, become the most feared arm of the government, similar to the Gestapo that existed in Nazi Germany in the nineteen-thirties and forties. They made things happen. People not aligned with the President often disappeared. No one wanted to be investigated by the CGSS or SS for short.

Colter had been a general in the Army. He had retired and joined Fergusson's campaign when he was first nominated by his party to run for President. He was the President's most trusted insider.

"Mister President," Colter said in greeting.

"Atwood, sit down."

Colter sat in a chair in front of Fergusson's desk.

Fergusson leaned back and said, "I need a few ideas about a problem."

Colter nodded.

"This homeless situation is out of control. Most of these homeless people are not ever going to be a contributing part of my country. I was wondering if you might have an idea about how to maybe reduce their numbers?"

"Reduce their numbers?" Colter responded questioningly; his eyes widened.

"To a more manageable level."

"Ah-huh?" Colter said, beginning to feel some discomfort. This suggestion was a bit extreme, even for Fergusson.

Fergusson didn't blink. He said, "I'm just fishing for some ideas."

"I have ideas but I'm not sure if this is a path we should go down."

"Let me be blunt, Colter. This is my country. I now own its future. My thought is that once the California location has been filled, maybe some kind of sickness happens that saves us the expense of continuing to maintain the city at these levels. Maybe we can ship the rest of the homeless to some other kind of camp, something not so expensive to maintain. Maybe something with tents. Besides, I like the city and think we can put it to better use. Maybe for scientific research to push us even farther ahead of the world."

Colter nodded then said, "First of all, you are just barely controlling the population as it is. People are afraid of your police but they also are not aware of how much freedom they have lost because most of them are insignificant and are still working. They know that their country has changed but they think it will, at some point, go back to the way it was. If they lose that hope because you do something that they find so egregious, they might just revolt in overwhelming numbers. That is something you couldn't put down, no matter how brutal you become. Leaders who end up in that situation find themselves hanging from a tree and blowing in the wind. Because of that, it's my opinion that we need to be more careful than we have been lately."

Fergusson paused at that and stared at Colter. He seemed as though he wanted to comment but refrained and changed the direction of the discussion. He said, "Also, Atwood, with the November elections coming up, I want to discuss how I can become the permanent leader of America since I can't run for office again."

"The Constitution is pretty air-tight about that, unless there was some desperate emergency. We don't want to become like Russia. Don't forget, you can also have some control out of office. Your wealth and the wealth of your family and allies are growing exponentially."

"I suppose," Fergusson replied. He wasn't happy with Colter's response. He loved being President and the power. He said, "An emergency, huh?"

Colter nodded then said, "Secondly, you need to realize that we are beginning to fall behind the world's more advanced countries."

Fergusson flared. He barked incredulously, "We are still the most advanced country."

"No, Sir, we are not. We have lost many of our best scientists and innovators. Most have moved to the Eurozone because of the loss of freedom here. Some have just disappeared. We think they may have quietly slipped into Mexico or Canada. Since your crackdown on the citizens in America, there has been a flight of talent as the state-run facilities and universities have become more repressive. Also, you have largely removed any incentive for these talented people to continue to innovate because of fear. As a matter of fact, Sir, you have had too many people imprisoned who these bright people looked up to, and even a few secretly killed, so, the ones remaining here, who don't have the means or connections to leave, just lay low and do enough to get by. No one wants to be noticed. Also, you have installed too many friends and associates in positions where they have no expertise so even if a significant discovery is made, they are too dumb to realize it. When you made the decision to use people who were loyal to you instead of people who were talented, you destroyed the structure that it takes to bring the discoveries from the drawing board to fruition. Because people are afraid, they do not innovate on their own. They are too busy hoping to survive. At some point, you must stop much of these practices or we will soon be a third-world country."

Fergusson's face was turning beet red. He began to splutter, "I have made this country far better than it would have ever been without me."

Colter breathed out, kept his expression flat, and continued, "I have been your man, Mister President, but I will never lie to you. You have alienated Great Britain which has strengthened its ties with the rest of the Eurozone because they now fear us. France and Germany are close to cutting diplomatic ties with us altogether. Israel has become much closer to Europe also and is exchanging technological breakthroughs with them. India is up and coming and has just approached Europe to become the newest member of its economic zone. China had moved slightly ahead of us because of all the technology that they were able to steal, but because they also have a repressive regime, like us, they do not have the innovators to push them forward. They will soon fall farther behind Europe who is now the only thing holding them in check. Because no less than 50 former American scientists and innovators have joined universities all over Europe, Europe will soon accelerate the technological gap between us and them. That's what freedom does. It makes people free to think, dream, and innovate. We still have notable wealth but it is being drained by our deep recession. Europe, as of now, is no longer in recession and all of our major technology corporations have moved important staff to their European headquarters. The CEOs and executives and their families, all stay in Europe full-time and never come back to America for fear of being arrested. Because Russia is much like us and China in their repressive regimes, and because of their institutionalized corruption, they were never able to fully catch up to us or China technologically, so they are quickly falling even farther behind the rest of the world. I would say that they could now be considered third-world. People think of Russia as a great power, but their economy is no bigger than Italy's."

"When did this begin happening and why didn't you inform me of this?"

"At first, it wasn't so easy to see as most of these executives have residences in other countries but as what was happening became evident to me, I did inform you when the first several scientist and executives began permanently leaving and then later when the trickle became a stream, but you brushed it off as not important. Not one of our top scientists or corporate leaders in biotech or technology companies, public or private, live in or come to the United States anymore. I believe that you said that they need us more than we need them. That might have been an overstatement. Most executives in energy and retail still reside here but not all and the number of them is shrinking. Both the Exxon and Chevron CEOs have just moved from the US."

Fergusson was speechless and Colter's expression remained flat. After a few uncomfortable seconds, Fergusson said, "I need to think. Get back to me with the homeless solution."

Colter bowed slightly, turned, and walked from the room.

Chapter 16

Homeless City

Hanna and Trish sat together on the train heading home from their second day of work. Both were tired.

Hanna sat by the window and watched as the lights passed while Trish stared forward barely able to keep her eyes open. Neither spoke.

The train stopped and several people got off. A few others came on. The train was beginning to mostly empty as riders from their work downtown reached their residences. It was now just a couple of stops from Hanna and Trish's apartment complex.

A man who had stepped into the car from the stop sat on a seat just behind Hanna and Trish. He was lean with an athletic frame, appeared to be just over six feet in height, and had a beard that looked like a two-month growth.

He stood then leaned down to Trish and quietly asked, "Hello. Could I bother you to change seats with me for a minute?"

She glanced up surprised.

His eyes and smile were warm.

Hanna glanced up also and instantly recognized John Black, the guy from the library.

Trish looked over at Hanna and said questioningly, "Hanna?"

Hanna nodded and said, "It's okay, Trish."

Trish got up and Jack, AKA, John Black, sat down next to Hanna.

He dumbly said, "Hi?"

"Hi?" Hanna repeated and began to chuckle. "Hi? Really?" She shook her head. "So, you do remember me?"

"Ah, yeah. Of course," Jack said.

"So... What are you doing here? And why the spy stuff at the library?" Hanna asked, cocked her head as she examined Jack's face, then commented, "I like you in the beard. It should be cut a bit closer, though."

Jack half-smiled and said, "Hanna, I'm so happy to see you."

"Really, you could have fooled me."

"I know. There's a reason that I acted like that at the library. I have so much to tell you. There's a lot that you don't know about me."

"Huh?"

"I've missed you, Hanna. I thought about you all the time."

Hanna glanced at Jack, looking for some deceit in his eyes. "Forgive me, but I find that hard to believe."

"I never thought I would ever see you again. I couldn't believe that you were in the library. Can we talk?"

"Isn't that what we're doing?"

Jack leaned in and whispered, "I can't be overheard when we talk."

"Geez, Jack, this is the wrong city to try to do anything in secret. There're cameras everywhere. In my room and even in my bathroom. I can't change or take a pee without someone watching. I feel like half the world has seen me naked. There are at least four cameras on this train car."

"You're right and they all have microphones but they're not all being monitored at one time. They don't have the manpower to do that but if they become suspicious of someone, I'm sure that you couldn't sneeze without them knowing. There are a few places where we can talk. I'll come to the library and let you know when we can meet and where."

"I work six twelve-hour days."

"I know."

"You do?"

"Yes. I'll figure it out."

The train stopped at the stop just before Hanna's apartment complex. Jack stood and walked out of the train's doors. They slid shut and the train started forward. Trish jumped up and sat back with Hanna.

"What the heck was that?" she exclaimed.

"I'm not really sure? I guess I'll find out."

"Handsome guy," Trish commented, looking sideways at Hanna.

"Yep."

They both sat back as the train picked up speed for their stop.

Chapter 17

Outside of Homeless City

In the long-abandoned military base outside of Homeless City, Jose Garza woke early not feeling quite right. He was having trouble breathing. He reached up and felt his forehead. It was on fire. Fever, he thought. Caught something. His next thought was, I'm a long way from a doctor.

Like all of the workers on the Homeless City project, Garza slept in a building in the abandoned military base in a barracks-like setting with rows of cots under sleeping bags. They all ate in a group with three good meals being provided but any need for serious medical attention would be provided in one of the infirmaries at Homeless City.

He rose from his cot and glanced around. No one else he could see was awake. The sun hadn't come up yet. He stood shakily and walked to the bathroom. As he entered, Chuck Green was standing at the sink and splashing water on his face.

"Hey, Chuck," Garza said, stepping to the urinal.

Green said, "Damn, man, I'm sick as a dog."

"You, too?"

"Shit. I got body aches and chills so bad my bones are shaking."

"Me too. We better let Ravello know. He's going to be pissed. He was pushing hard to get that last phase finished."

"Tough shit. I can barely stand, let alone work. He's going to need to get us to the doctor."

Green walked out of the restroom first and down a short hallway where Vincent Ravello had a private separate room. He banged on his door.

"Just a minute," Ravello answered.

Ravello opened the door and saw Green standing there.

"What is it?"

"I'm sick Boss. Real sick. I think I need to see a doctor."

Ravello nodded and said, "I'm not feeling so well either. I hope our cooks didn't poison us. Maybe it will pass."

"I just saw Garza in the head and he's bad as me."

"Shit. This job ain't going to get done this way. Alright, let's get everyone up and see if anyone else is sick. We can take a bus into the city and see some of their docs."

They woke the work crews and at least twenty of the two hundred or so now left on the construction crew were displaying similar symptoms. They boarded one of the busses that brought them to the worksite and headed to the city. The sun was just beginning to rise on the eastern hills and it lit the sky with orange and red.

When they arrived in the city, they drove down the main street to East Infirmary. Lights that came on when the sun went down were beginning to wink out.

As they drove up to the infirmary, they could see a large line of people, all dressed in grey jumpsuits, standing in front of the doors to the medical building.

"What's this?" Ravello said questioningly.

"Something's wrong, Boss," Garza said, sitting near Ravello.

The bus stopped and Ravello got off and walked to the front of the line where two nurses in scrubs, masks, and face shields stood with clipboards questioning the first few sick in line.

Ravello said, "Excuse me. I have a busload of guys from the construction site who are all sick. Can you see them?"

"We're overrun here. We are sending people to the infirmary at the Asylum. Take the boulevard to twelfth street."

Ravello nodded and walked back to the bus. He boarded and told the driver where to go.

They drove the next eight blocks to twelfth street and turned right. They then drove a couple of blocks and the street ended at a cyclone gate that allowed entry into the Asylum. The Asylum was surrounded by a twelve-foot cement wall. Citizen Guards stood at the gate.

When the bus pulled up, two guards outside the gate walked out of a small security guardhouse.

The first Guard said, "What's your business?"

The bus driver spoke through his window, "I got a busload of sick guys in here. We were sent to your infirmary from the Eastern Medical Facility. They are too busy to help."

The guard nodded and walked back to his small security booth, made a call, then walked back to the bus. He said, "The infirmary is straight ahead, two blocks on the left." He then stepped back and opened the gate. The bus pulled forward.

After three hours of seeing the Asylum doctors, the construction workers were released with the diagnosis that they had contracted a flu of some kind.

Chapter 18

Homeless City

Eastern Library

At 8:50 pm, the next day, Hanna kept glancing at the clock. The day had been slow. Though Homeless City was filling up, people were getting jobs and fewer were coming to the library.

All she could think about was seeing Jack again. She had hoped that he would come to the library today but he didn't actually say that he would come, *today*, just that he would come.

She sighed.

Trish glanced over at her and seeing the look on her face, asked, "You okay?"

"Yeah."

When 9:00 pm arrived, everyone met at the door and filed out. They walked as a group down the stairs and talked together towards the trains.

Trish said, "I'm beat. Twelve hours on the job is too long."

Hanna responded, "Yeah, they want us busy and tired. People are far more manageable that way."

"That's true," came a voice from behind Hanna.

She turned to see Jack.

He smiled through a much shorter beard, now no more than three days growth. Then he continued,

"Trish, do you mind if I steal Hanna away from you? We have a few things to discuss."

"I guess?" Trish replied unsurely.

Hanna turned to Trish and said, "I'll see you tomorrow."

Trish nodded and walked towards the train platform.

Jack turned to Hanna and said questioningly, "Walk with me?"

She nodded and they walked back up the steps and out into the evening.

The night was warm and clear and a mild breeze had arisen from south of Homeless City. The Moon was nearly full, blotting out all but the brightest stars.

Jack said, "This way."

They walked around a corner and to a maintenance door beside the library. Jack waved the back of his hand over a keypad by the door and it unlocked with an audible click. The normal vocal response did not occur from the security device on the door.

"In here."

"Won't someone see us?"

"No. I've disabled all the cameras that can view this small maintenance closet. They'll be working to fix the problem but it'll take them at least a couple of hours. Come on. Inside."

Hanna gave Jack a confused look then stepped into the closet. It was around five feet by ten feet. There were a few garbage cans and carts to move items, some cleaning supplies, brooms, and dustpans, but nothing more. Though the cans were clean, the closet still had a slight garbage scent.

Jack waved his left hand over a switch on the wall and a dim light lit the small space.

"What's with the magic hand-waving thing?"

"So, when I tell you my story, you'll understand more about me. I have a device built into my left index finger. It just looks like the bone if it's x-rayed. It gives off an RFID signal like a credit card, but it's a powerful computer that has some advanced technology built into it that allows me certain access into different things. I created it myself. It's not government-issued. Most of the maintenance workers use RFID cards to operate the locks and lights in the city."

"Huh?" Hanna said mystified. Then she smiled and added, "Just like old times during our affair, Jack, sneaking around. Though, we never ended up in a place so... what's the word I'm looking for... odoriferous."

Jack smiled and glanced at the floor. "Best I could do on short notice."

Hanna smiled.

Jack continued, "I take it, you are no longer married?"

"Nope. I'm a single lady. When I knew you, I was on my first marriage. That ended and I married again but that didn't work out either."

"I always had the feeling that you wouldn't be happy that way, not being married, I mean."

"No," she said, breathing out. "I have never wanted to be alone but no one knows better than you that I'm not so good at fidelity or relationships."

"You always seemed restless, Hanna." He made that statement with a great deal of affection, though the words were not complementary.

"An obvious character flaw. I've never been happy with one man for very long and I've never been happy in one place." Hanna shrugged and glanced into Jack's eyes. She looked away then continued, "I don't know why. I've been with men that I really liked and was sometimes truly in love with but it never seemed like enough. My mind would wander and eventually, so would I."

"So, if you and I would have gotten together back then, you think you wouldn't have been faithful to me?"

"I don't know, for sure, Jack. I was very much in love with you. It did seem different. You seemed like the perfect man for me. I would have left my husband for you but we probably would have had to have a discussion about the flaws in me that you clearly construed." She paused. "I cried for weeks after you left, you know. I couldn't get over it."

"Can I hug you, Hanna? I've wanted to hug you for a very long time."

Hanna nodded and they came close together. Standing in the middle of a closet filled with cleaning supplies, they embraced. Neither wanted to separate... Minutes passed... Neither spoke.

Hanna felt her body pressed tightly against Jack's. She could feel his hard chest, stomach, and legs. Her arms rubbed his muscular back and shoulders. She could feel his hands trace her back.

She pushed back and said, "You feel like you've kept yourself in good shape. Your body feels good." She smiled and rubbed the outsides of his arms. They felt like steel.

"I have had to. My job makes it necessary for me to be at a peak performance level."

"What are you, an Olympic athlete?"

"This is where my story gets harder to explain. You have to promise me that you won't discuss this with anyone. My life depends on it."

"Are you in trouble?"

"Yeah, you might say that."

Hanna paused for a minute looking into Jack's eyes then she said, "Jack, why don't you get to the point? Why did you want to see me?"

Jack sighed, "Because I fell in love with you all those years ago. When I saw you in the library, I couldn't believe it."

"So, why didn't you come back to me back then, when you could?"

"My work is dangerous and anyone who would have been with me, back then, might have been in danger. They use people that you know to get to you. I have a lot of enemies both in-country and out."

"You told me that you were in the military."

"Not exactly."

"What exactly do you do?"

Jack breathed out. "I'm a government employee. At least I was. I deal with other people that are like me and are enemies of our country. I primarily write code for operating systems that allow us backdoors into computers, so that we can spy on our enemies. So, I hack."

"That doesn't sound that bad. Not if you're working for the government."

Jack rubbed his face. "Listen, Hanna. That's not all I do. I've done some terrible things. I do very specialized work besides the hacking."

"So, you're saying that you are some kind of assassin?"

He nodded, and paused for a couple of heartbeats, then continued, "But, at least it was against our enemies, then our government was more or less, taken over by Fergusson. It was crazy how he used the laws and his power to make enough changes to get more control. I was put under the authority of his Gestapo. Did you know that they secretly call themselves SS? Like from Nazi Germany? Assholes. My boss, Atwood Colter, back at Langley, began asking me to do things to citizens of the United States. These were just people who didn't agree with President Fergusson. I refused and caught flack."

"How long have you been homeless?"

"Nearly three years now."

"That's a long time."

Jack nodded then continued the story, "It took a while for me to figure out what was going on. I was busy doing my job. Fergusson was a bad guy right out of the gate but he progressively got worse. Because I can hack into any system, I began watching what people were saying about me. I found out that Colter, the head of the SS, had me scheduled for permanent termination. Not the kind with a pension, the kind in a box. So, I disappeared and became a ghost. They knew that I was dangerous and could make life miserable for some of them if I chose to. So, instead, I purposely became homeless and blended into the mass of homeless humanity. I thought about taking the war to them. I could take a lot of them down before they got me but I chose to disappear instead. I got caught in a homeless round-up. I had already scrubbed every way that the authorities could identify me and became John Black. I even altered the facial recognition file that they have on me. I could have gotten away but I thought that this city might not be a bad place to end up. I'd be right under their noses and once I established a way into the city's computer systems, I could always stay one step ahead of them and hike if I needed to. A few in my business could visually identify me but they would have to see me. I sent them all looking for ghosts all over the world. To give them credit, they've turned over every stone that they thought that I crawled under. They think that I'm somewhere in Europe right now, like a lot of Americans who figured out early what Fergusson was about."

"Huh?" Hanna replied, not quite knowing how to handle what she had been told. She asked, "What is Fergusson about?"

"That guy's a piece of work. He's pretty bad on the surface but the reality is far worse than just what you see. He's a megalomaniac and a sociopath, not to mention, a pathological liar. I've figured out, between the lines, that he never plans to leave office and I think he wants his family to rule after him. Colter might not even know that. Fergusson only barely holds the country together, as it is, so he teeters on the constant threat that the country will implode and he'll end up on the end of a rope, swinging in the breeze. After he gains complete power, he would never allow our constitution to be reestablished. I think he plans to pull a Hitler with the help of the Supreme Court, the Attorney General, and the Senate. Game, set, match. All the people who should stop him are somehow missing the big picture because they care more about petty short-term political gains than they do about the constitution of the United States and our people. They think that they can handle Fergusson but they're wrong. Fergusson has already begun a war of terror on his political enemies and even on his allies who he thinks have too much power and influence. He has sent them all scurrying for cover like roaches after the lights go on. As soon as he gets control, he'll wage war on anything standing in his path of total power. He will replace judges and members of the Senet and House who are not loyal to him. This guy Colter is the brains behind Fergusson. I don't think Fergusson could think his way out of a wet paper bag but he's ruthless. I doubt that Fergusson does anything without checking with Colter first but Colter doesn't control Fergusson. Fergusson is too volatile and unpredictable. Colter is also ruthless but rational. I think Colter just barely keeps Fergusson from full-on madness."

"So, how do you fit into this?"

"At first, I continued to do my work. Sometimes it's hard to see the forest because all the trees are in the way. My superiors would point me in the direction of people who were supposed to be legitimate targets and I would do what I do."

"So, they were pointing you at political enemies?"

"All of the traditional targets in Russia, North Korea, China, and the Middle East, for some reason, became unimportant. Targets who I had been working for years to neutralize were suddenly off the table and the only targets remaining were American citizens."

"So, you killed these people?"

"Mostly not."

"Then what?"

"It depended on the case. I wouldn't kill the Americans and also mostly not the enemies. Sometimes I would send them off in the wrong direction to slow them down so I could eventually catch up with them. Mostly, I would plant misinformation to discredit the individual, fake crimes, and the like, you know, character assassination. If you do it right, you get them locked up for something unrelated. I did this to several Americans who they had me set up to be arrested. They planted some misinformation to make me think that I was helping to get rid of bad guys, but they weren't. These were guys from both parties, so I was slow to catch on. I became suspicious after they wanted me to set up someone who I was pretty sure was a good guy, so, I started to do my own research no matter what Colter would give me and I found out that he was feeding me bullshit."

"But you killed other people?"

"Oh yeah. If it was someone who had done significant damage to America in some way. These were mostly terrorists and assassins. Those guys are hard to get to using normal channels. By hacking, I've caused a couple of accidents. I've also done wet work, finding these guys and permanently ending their careers. Sometimes it would take months to get someone alone enough so I wouldn't hurt an innocent. Fergusson doesn't care about collateral damage, though."

Jack glanced down at the floor, then rubbed his face and looked back into Hanna's eyes. "I've also had to kill to defend myself. I've been hunted by these same people who have no problem killing. That's what they do and sometimes they make it as slow and cruel as possible. They like to send messages."

"So, what now, Jack? What's the plan?"

He breathed out thinking that he had said too much. “For now, my plan is to live between the cracks for a while and hopefully outlive these assholes but I don’t know.” He paused and rubbed his chin, then said, “You should go.”

“Will I see you again?”

“I think so. If you want to. I’ve probably told you too much. Do you want to see me again?”

“Well, I don’t know. I have a very busy social calendar. Ummm...”

Jack interrupted, “I’ve missed you, Hanna. I’ve missed you, so much.”

Hanna half-smiled and softly kissed Jack’s lips. She said, “Get me out of this closet, Jack.”

He nodded and smiled, then turned and cracked the door, checking to make sure that no one was outside. He opened it slowly and they slipped out, heading back to the trains.

Before they separated, Hanna said, “I want to see you again, Jack. I don’t know exactly how to proceed from here but I want to see you again.”

Jack nodded and smiled, “I’ll be in touch.” He turned and walked away.

Hanna caught the train for home.

Chapter 19

Homeless City

At noon the next day, Jack Morgan, AKA, John Black, slipped into a small office near the eastern entrance to Homeless City. He knew that he had but a short time before the workers would return. Jack had been watching this office for three days and each day, the two who worked here left for lunch at exactly this time. They would need to take the train to the cafeteria then eat and return. He had a little under an hour.

Jack rummaged around the office, opening drawers, and found several flash drives. He took one that was no bigger than half a dime.

He then sat down at one of the computer stations. The computer was on but in standby mode. He touched the keyboard and the monitor lit with the password screen. When it came up, he typed in his master password, and like magic, he had access to the computer.

He then inserted the flash drive into the computer port and then programmed it using its RFID signal to communicate with the device that Jack had surgically inserted under the skin of his index finger. The flash drive would give him the ability to collect data and because it was programmed for use in the city, possibly some other covert uses.

He typed in several commands then waited for his own secret account to come up. It lay embedded in every government operating system. His fingers danced on the keyboard. This was the second time he had been in the city's computer systems but the first time, someone had returned early and he couldn't complete his tasks.

At that time, he pulled up a program called "Tracing." When the program came up, a mapped grid of the city appeared and thousands of tiny number/letter sequences surrounded in black, red, blue, or green moved like ants inside the grid. Jack figured out that each number/letter sequence was a person living in the city and the colors denoted where each person was currently housed. The black was everywhere and must be guards and employees of Homeless City, the red were only in the Asylum, the blue only in the Rehab Center, and the green were scattered throughout the city and must be the residents not condemned to the Asylum or the Rehab Center. There were a few green number/letter sequences in the Asylum. All of those were stationary.

Once in this time, he reestablished himself as one of the system's administrators for all of the computer systems in Homeless City. From here, he could control specific things in the city or leave brief digital tracks all over Europe. He had done this many times in the past, before coming to the city, using computers in libraries and from laptops in public places and made those looking for him so sure that they had found him, that they sent the black helicopters only to discover that it was a wild goose chase. If they ever caught him, though, there'd be hell to pay, but for now, he was the one pulling the strings and they knew it.

He then pulled up the recorded camera images, removing the recording of him entering this office and replacing it with the recordings from an hour earlier. He turned off the cameras and set them to restart in ten minutes. Now, he could see what was going on.

He looked through the government's databases relating to him and they continued to look for him in Europe. He then glanced around for Homeless City's administrator. He couldn't be called a mayor. There he was, Karl Archer. He found communiques from the White House asking mundane questions about the current number of homeless now residing in the city. Jack was surprised to see that it was approaching 900,000. He pulled up a blueprint of the city. It was spread out for thirty square miles and had a large portion for housing the addicted homeless to get them off of whatever they were addicted to. Then he perused the Asylum. He was surprised to see that it had been built one story above ground, but another five stories underground. No other building was constructed so, though, there was an extensive underground transportation system. Through camera feeds, he perused the hallways on each floor and then looked into several rooms. The rooms were stark with one bed and a toilet in a corner. The inmates in the rooms either sat or laid on the beds staring into space. Some were restrained. Most appeared to be desolate. He had seen some terrible things in his life but there was something so disturbing about the expressions on these inmates' faces that it left him chilled.

He glanced at the clock. Two more minutes. He went to the electronic correspondence and found an email from Atwood Colter. It was from two days ago.

"Huh?" he said to himself then thought, why would Colter be communicating with anyone here?

He pulled it up.

Karl Archer

April 14, 2038

We need to discuss further the concerns that I spoke to you about yesterday. This is of the utmost importance to DF. I will call you on the secure line tomorrow at noon.

Colter

"Huh?" Jack said aloud. Then thought, I'd love to have heard that call but it was yesterday. Who is DF? Could be Donald Fergusson. Who else.

He glanced at the clock on the computer. Time to go. He dragged several items into the storage on the flash drive including several emails then returned the computer to where it was when he arrived, scrubbed any record that someone had been in this computer, shut down his account, pulled the flash drive, and walked out of the building checking for people on the streets.

As usual, the streets were deserted, so he quickly walked around the corner, down the block, and into the crowded underground train stop closest to the office that he had just left. He had stopped all of the cameras from recording to this point. He glanced at a clock by the trains. Under a minute until all the cameras returned to normal and began recording the streets and the office where he had just been.

From the middle of the pack of people waiting for their ride, he stood and waited as the train came to a stop. The door to the train opened and he slipped into the train car and it pulled out, heading back to his home. As he rode, he thought about Atwood Colter, the head of the CGSS. A bit of paranoia leaked into Jack's thinking. Had Colter suspected that he was in Homeless City? Probably not or he would have already been apprehended. So, why was he needing to communicate with Archer?

Jack thought about his situation. He was going to need access to a computer on a more regular basis.

The next day, Jack approached a supply warehouse that was bringing on workers because of the overwhelming need to feed, clothe, and supply the growing population.

Jack walked into the warehouse. It was an open space with high open ceilings, loading docks, and homeless residents driving forklifts and tow motors as they unloaded pallets from trucks that lined the docks. It was a massive operation.

Jack approached one of the black-clad workers holding a clipboard and looking stressed. He appeared to be a foreman of some kind and was checking-in the deliveries and directing the forklift drivers.

"Hi," Jack said, walking up. The guy didn't look up from his clipboard.

"I was wondering if you could use some help in this warehouse. I haven't been placed in a job yet. This looks like something that I can do."

The guy then glanced up and said, "See Micky." He pointed towards an office. "Over there."

"Thanks," Jack replied and turned and walked to the office. He approached the door and peeked inside. An African American man was sitting behind a small desk. He appeared to be in his early fifties with greying hair.

He glanced up from glaring at his computer monitor and said, "Yes."

Jack said, "You Micky?"

"Yeah."

"I'm looking for work. I haven't been placed yet."

"Can you drive a forklift?"

"Sure can."

"Got any computer skills?"

"A few."

"Have your social worker send over your paperwork. We're not keeping up here. I need more help. Here's my card. Tell him or her that I need lots more help. I'm sure they will put you on."

"Great. Thanks."

Jack walked from the warehouse and out into a warm day. He glanced at the empty streets. No one walked there. He walked back towards his small room and past one of the infirmaries. People were lined out of the doors. They all appeared to be pretty sick. He wondered about that but these were homeless people and probably not in the best of health, to begin with.

When he got back to his room, he used the wall phone to contact his social worker. The phone had several buttons that only allowed contact to the social worker, the infirmary, the Citizen Guard security, and to an operator. He pushed his social worker's button and got a voice mail where he left a message.

Chapter 20

Washington DC

The Oval Office

Atwood Colter arrived at the White House. He checked in with security, walked to the Oval Office, and was announced in.

President Fergusson sat behind his desk and watched as Colter entered.

Colter approached the desk.

"Well?" Fergusson barked abruptly.

"Sir, I want to again caution you against this policy. Once you start down this road, there is no going back."

"Don't you think I know it, Colter? Look at what we have already done. This isn't going to make a bit of difference if my government falls. Besides, I am making this country far better with my policies. Even this one. You know that these people are mostly worthless. So, Colter, what's the plan?"

"I have contacted someone who I have total trust in. This person has spent most of his adult life working in biowarfare. He says that there is a strain of Legionnaires disease that does not spread from person to person. It would need to be injected but if an autopsy were performed on a deceased individual, it would appear that the person contracted the disease in the normal fashion through filtration systems. He believes that it would be impossible to link it to the injection. The people would die at different rates so it wouldn't appear as a mass murder but would appear like the spread of a pandemic. This strain isn't contagious so the spread will be controlled and won't slip out into the general population. He says that each injection would have different viral loads so people wouldn't all become sick at once. No one would get sick in the first week. The onset of the symptoms would begin at the start of the second week and would increase in severity in around two weeks from the time of the injections with the deaths beginning in the third week and continuing through the fourth week and a bit longer. At that point, most of the infected will die. Some will not as their immune systems will be able to fight off the disease. You could begin evacuating some of the people to the camps that you had mentioned before. I'm sure you would have no trouble playing it up and making yourself a hero for acting quickly to save their lives." Colter smiled at the obvious sarcasm.

The sarcasm went right over Fergusson's head, though, as he thought about the substance of Colter's message.

"What excuse are you going to use for the injections?"

"Flu vaccine."

"Do it. What will it take?"

My contact says that he has access to the vials. We switch our vials with the flu vaccine scheduled to be shipped to the city. None of the doctors on-site will have any idea what they are administering. Most of the doctors and nurses will probably administer the vaccine to themselves so they will also die at some point making the problem worsen. We can't have anyone with a conscience knowing about this. I'll personally handle the shipment switch. My contact will handle the labeling of the vials."

"Do it."

"Okay?"

Colter turned and walked from the room. He had an odd sense of just selling his soul to the Devil but the fact of the matter was that he had sold it long ago.

Chapter 21

Truckloads of cement and dirt arrived near the border of Mexico and the coastal city of Long Beach in Southern California from the desert, removed from the excavation of Homeless City. The cement and dirt were to be used as landfill for a project in Long Beach to extend the military base located there and for a new luxury hotel to be built just across the border in Mexico.

The dirt and cement were then dumped, partially on land and partially in the water. Arriving with the dirt and cement was the mold from the underground room, and two days later, people around the dumping sites started to become sick. The spores from the mold from the desert cement blew inland on the ocean breeze and when it was inhaled by the construction workers and residents, they began coughing and some, who had inhaled copious amounts, needed to be rushed to an emergency room.

Within three days, the emergency rooms close to the sites were overrun. The attending physicians were baffled by the sudden onset of this respiratory illness and had no idea that the same illness was striking people in the still-secret Homeless City. They began testing to try to find out what was causing the illness but the tests were inconclusive and not showing any virus or bacteria that could be responsible. The illness was spreading, though, and the supply of ventilators was running thin.

Chapter 22

Homeless City

The day at the library was not normal. Hanna noticed that nearly every person walking in the doors was coughing. She glanced at Trish who was checking out a book for a patron. Trish appeared flushed and beads of sweat had gathered on her brow.

"Hey, Trish? Are you alright?"

"I don't think so,'" she said and began coughing.

"Do you want to go sit down?"

"Yeah. I'll be back in a few minutes."

Trish walked from her computer and towards the breakroom.

Hanna helped the next few people then saw Trish return towards the checkout counter. She was coughing. She stopped in mid-step and seemed to wobble.

Hanna rushed from behind the counter to Trish.

"Trish?"

Trish glanced at Hanna but her eyes didn't seem to focus.

"Huh?" she responded.

"You need to go to the doctor."

"Yeah. I think so."

The head librarian, Ann Voss, walked by the checkout counter and saw Hanna talking to Trish.

Voss walked up and said, "What's up?"

Hanna responded, “Trish is really sick. I think she needs to see a doctor.”

Voss took one look a Trish and said, “She doesn’t look well. Come on, Trish. I’ll walk you to the infirmary. It’s just down the block.”

Trish nodded and she and Voss walked from the library.

Twenty minutes later, Voss returned.

Hanna saw her entering the front door and approached her. “How’s Trish?”

“I got her in to see the doctor. She didn’t look good. They're taking her someplace where she will get better care.”

Hanna shook her head. “Oh,” she commented, then turned, and walked back to her station.

At 9:05 pm, Hanna stood at the double doors waiting for everyone working to gather then leave for the night. All she could think about for the rest of her shift was Trish. She wanted to go to her but she had no idea where to find her.

The last patron had left fifteen minutes earlier and Ann Voss had needed to stop by her office for a minute.

She returned to the front doors and said, “Okay. Let’s go.”

Everyone stepped out of the double doors and said goodbye.

Voss locked the doors behind her and said, “See you in the morning.”

Voss turned and walked away towards her apartment that was close to the library and much nicer than anything the homeless residents had been given. She was coughing.

Hanna walked down the steps to the train platform worrying about Trish and also thinking about Jack. She didn't know if she would ever see him again. There was just no way to communicate with him.

Her train arrived and she began walking onto the car as the doors opened. She sat and a man came up and sat down beside her.

"Hi," he said.

Hanna turned, startled, "Jack?! Where'd you come from?"

"Around."

"I haven't seen you for a week."

"I've been a bit busy."

"Doing what?"

"Poking around."

"What are you poking at?"

Several people on the bus were coughing in the background.

"Well, there are a lot of people sick here. Really sick. The infirmaries are overflowing. How are you feeling?"

"Okay. I have a bit of a cough but Trish had to leave work today and go to the doctor. She looked awful. How are you?"

"Like you, a bit of a cough, but nothing more. I did some digging and they are saying that it's some kind of respiratory virus like the flu. Maybe it's the flu, but I don't know. I saw a communique that said that they are rushing some kind of vaccine to the city."

"That sounds positive, but you sound skeptical?"

"I don't know. The timing of the communique didn't seem right. It was too early for them to react so quickly to rush a vaccine here. I don't get it. It might just be that I don't trust anyone right now, but I am suspicious. I'll do more digging. It looks like a lot of people are going to die from this sickness. I'm worried. A few people are already on ventilators. Some of those infected don't seem to be that bad, but some affected are extremely sick. The symptoms seem to vary."

Concern showed on Hanna's face and she nodded but then said, "I'm glad to see you, Jack." She glanced up into his eyes.

"Me too."

"Are you working yet?"

"No, but I have a line on a job that should be what I've been looking for."

"Looking for?"

"I'll explain later."

"Later?"

"Yep," Jack replied shortly then said, "Will you come to my place tonight?"

"I don't know. You seem like trouble."

"Are you kidding?"

"Of course, dummy. Let's go."

"We need to get off at the next stop."

"Okay."

The train stopped and they got off and walked without too much discussion towards Jack's apartment. Hanna took his hand.

He turned and smiled.

They reached his door and it unlocked. "John Black," came from the security device on the door.

Hanna whispered, "No wavy-hand-thing?"

"I don't need it here."

She nodded and they walked inside.

The lights came on and Hanna said, "I like what you've done with the place."

"It's my interior decorator. She's a genius."

He turned and pulled Hanna into his arms and kissed her hard. She kissed him back and her pulse and breathing became rapid.

He reached for her breast and she said, "You don't honestly think that I would jump back in bed with you?"

"I was hoping."

"Huh? But what about my virtue?"

"Well, that is something to think about."

Hanna put her arms around Jack and kissed him urgently then unzipped his grey jumpsuit. "Screw my virtue."

Jack pushed her jumpsuit off of her shoulders and pulled off her bra. He kissed both breasts then pushed the jumpsuit below her hips and she pushed his jumpsuit below his. They stopped and fumbled off the rest of their clothes, pulling off their shoes and socks, and both laughed at their clumsiness. Finally nude, Jack pulled Hanna onto his small bed and rolled on top of her. She took hold of him and hastily pushed him into her and they began moving together. They gripped each other tightly and kissed.

Hanna gasped breathlessly as they moved, finding a once forgotten rhythm. She wrapped both legs around him and rocked her hips to meet each stroke.

When they'd finished, they lay sweating together in Jack's bed.

"So much for foreplay," Hanna commented wryly.

"Next time."

"I wonder how many people watched us just now?" Hanna said questioningly.

"None. I've turned the cameras off in the rooms in this housing block and a few of the others away from here for the last two hours. They're probably working to fix the problem but they won't be able to. They will restart on their own."

"That waving-hand thing is useful. Would you mind waving it when I'm in the showers and also maybe when I need to use the restroom? It's disconcerting to think that someone's peering at me while in a private moment."

"Like a few minutes ago?"

"Well, yeah, as a matter of fact, I prefer my orgasms to be private."

Jack smiled, "I actually did it on a computer. I set it up to give us some privacy."

"You were pretty sure of yourself."

Jack smiled and spooned Hanna to him. He said, "There hasn't been a day go by where I haven't thought of you. It didn't matter what I was doing and you would unexpectantly pop into my mind. I missed our conversations and I never thought I would see you again, and honestly, I never thought I would get to enjoy your kiss again. I've thought a lot about your kiss."

"Just my kiss?"

"Mostly."

"Not the sex?"

"Well, of course, but I can't describe your kiss. It communicates so much." Jack paused for a second then said wistfully, "God, I did miss that kiss."

"Mmmm," Hanna said then pulled him into another kiss. She pushed Jack to his back and stated,

"I've missed things about you too, Jack." She smiled playfully and took him into her hand, again, and he rose to her. She pushed him back inside her and she took her pleasure until they both reached again. "Ohhh," she sighed, breathing out. "I so needed a good shagging."

Jack smiled then chuckled.

Hanna flopped off him and onto the bed, pulling his arm around her, and bringing his hand up to cup her breast. She snuggled her backside to him and asked, "Do you work tomorrow?"

"I'm checking into a job. I'm first laying some groundwork in their computers to make me seem more... What's the word I'm looking for? Ah, indispensable. I'm going to slow their computers to a walk."

"You are a bit scary, you know."

"I tried to tell you that... So, Hanna, how did you end up here? You're way too sharp to be homeless. I don't get it."

"It's kind of a long, sordid story."

"Well, since I'm lying in bed with you, we've made love twice, so far, and I currently have no clothes on, I don't think I'm going anywhere. I think I can spare a bit of time."

"Some of the story, you already know. In my two divorces, I had never been married long enough to accumulate any assets or money, and no kids, so I mostly just left with the clothes on my back, a few trinkets, and a car. You already know that I have no family and I also had no close friends at the time to fall back on. I got a great job in an advertising agency and was making really good money. I mistakenly started dating my boss who was the CEO. That's never a good idea. He was like me, shallow, and not interested in too much bonding. It seemed like a good fit and what I was looking for. The guy had an unexpected kink, though. He liked sex in groups. I had no idea. We had been together for about three months and the sex, to that point, had been normal. He had a party at his penthouse with a group of big shots, all high-rollers, you know, a bunch of movers and shakers. Everyone there was high and drunk by the end of the night, including me. The party thinned to eight people, four men, and four women, which included me. That's when things got weird. Two of the women began dancing and taking off their clothes. The third woman who was there was more like me and had no idea what was going on. As each piece of clothing fell to the floor, the younger woman's eyes became wider and wider. She was also dating her boss. Once the first two women were undressed, the group began clapping and exhorting the younger woman to take off her clothes. It was the last thing she wanted to do. This girl was innocent, not like me," Hanna chuckled ironically then continued, "I had no interest in group sex but she was like, Midwest naive. Her boss made it clear that if she didn't cooperate, she was going nowhere. I was watching this strange scene unfold in a kind of slow motion. I was ripped, drunk, and high off my ass, but still aware enough. They made her strip with the help of the other two ladies, who this obviously wasn't their first rodeo. Then the girl, I shouldn't call her a girl but she wasn't more than twenty-two, had sex with her boss on a chair in front of everyone. She wasn't happy about it and it seemed to feed the sex frenzy. It wasn't just about sex; it was about power. They were getting off on the coercion. Then she was passed to this other creepy guy who did her on a couch. He purposely turned her so everyone could watch. No one there was wearing condoms. My boss was watching and had embraced me from behind and had my blouse unbuttoned. I had been so ripped and involved with watching the surreal scene before me that I barely knew that I was so exposed. But I did know that he was touching me intimately and I was allowing it. By this time, the other three couples were all hooked up in this wild sex scene. It's sometimes strange what you recall thinking back. I can see the young woman with tears on her cheeks and the way her body moved with each stroke. She made eye contact with me several times as this was going on and she appeared as if wanting to say, how did I get myself into this?" Hanna paused contemplatively then continued, "She was so pretty. She had long dark straight hair and she was fit as if she was an athlete. She looked so desolate. Later, I thought that I almost wished it was me rather than her being passed around. I knew that what was happening to her wouldn't break me but I wasn't so sure about her. I think she was going to be crushed by the experience. I didn't want to be involved in it but I'd have been able to get over it." Hanna paused, again, for a moment then continued, "It was so weird to be witnessing the bizarre scene first-hand. It was like being unattached to my own body, but the cloudy, smokey memory of it is even more strange and dreamlike. Anyway, I glanced down to see my boss rubbing my top and I was a little bit exposed if you know what I mean. By this time, I fully understood what was going on. I let him continue for a minute, trying to think of some kind of compromise in the situation that I found myself in, something in between the unacceptable portions of the strange turn of events, but I slurred that I wasn't interested in being passed around. That didn't make him happy. I guess that I wasn't so moral that I might not have had sex with him if he got me someplace not so visible. I knew that people would be able to see us, but I wasn't going to do the trading partners thing, for sure, and while I wasn't interested in everyone watching, if it was somewhat away from the group, I would have complied even if they could see. By this time, my boss was extremely aroused so I thought that I might be able to sidetrack him away and get it over with, but he wasn't interested in not being part of the orgy. So, at that point in the weird evening, I became a bit angry that he wanted me to perform in this thing that was going on. To make a long story a little shorter, I told him that I couldn't do this and I decided to leave. As I was leaving, he told me not to come to work on Monday and that my great job was gone. I didn't expect that. The economy was collapsing and there were few jobs to be had. The younger woman knew that of course. That's why she allowed herself to be passed around that night. I'm not judging her. I almost walked back when he told me I was out of a job. I mean I really considered it. I stopped and very nearly turned around. In my mind, I mentally consented. I was going to go back. Then, I pictured myself being passed around and ending up impaled on the slimeball on the couch, so, I kept walking. Monday came around and as promised, he fired me. I didn't think he would follow through with the threat but he did." Hanna paused for a moment then said, "I thought he cared for me, at least a little. I guess not."

She breathed out. "I searched for work for four months. No one was hiring. I thought he might call me back but he didn't. I had spent all the money that I had been making as fast as I earned it. I qualified for unemployment, but it was pennies compared to my rich lifestyle so I got behind on my rent and was nearly evicted. My lovely landlord offered me a cheaper apartment because I was so behind but it came with strings and I had no money. He used me one night. I didn't exactly consent but I didn't stop him either. I was already at rock bottom and drinking like a fish. In just four months, I had been broken to the point where I would trade sex for rent and I did. That first time, I was willing enough. I admit it. What a loser." Hanna paused for a moment and shook her head, then continued, "The next day he came back with a friend to "help me" move and they both raped me. They were wearing condoms so no DNA. That time I wasn't so willing. I tried to fight them off, but they held me down and took turns with me. I gave in then and did what they wanted to get rid of them. It lasted for a couple of hours. I wanted to go to the police but I didn't think I would be believed so I packed up everything I could carry, got in my expensive BMW, which I had just purchased a few months before with nearly all my savings, and drove off with no job, no savings, and no plan. And that's how you end up homeless."

Jack hadn't moved or uttered a sound in the entire monologue. Hanna turned to see if he had fallen asleep.

"Jack?"

She turned further and Jack's face was red. He had a look on it that you wouldn't want to be directed at you.

"What is it, Jack?"

"I may need to catch up with these bastards someday."

"No, Jack. I didn't tell you the story to get revenge on these assholes. They'll get what they deserve someday. It isn't that I've forgiven them. I haven't, but I've let it go. It isn't going to make me bitter. I also have to take some responsibility."

"You don't need to take responsibility for being raped."

"No, you're right. Not for that, but I mean for not planning ahead, not saving, and for not being financially ready. That I could have done, but I thought that the money would always roll in. I had made enough by that time to have a fat bank account but I lived high on the hog and didn't save."

"Still."

"I know... But I have hurt people, too... Bad, Jack. I wouldn't want to think that they were out there waiting to get revenge on me and that includes the husband who I was with when you and I were sneaking around."

Jack looked away guiltily.

"My landlord would have left that first time he wanted to have sex with me if I would have given him a firm no, but I didn't, then he and his friend wouldn't have come back the next night expecting me to comply. That's not a free pass for the asshole, though. It isn't an excuse. No should always mean no. He would have put me out on the street, though, and I had already lost my dream job because I wouldn't fuck my boss and his friends at that party. I had been drinking heavily, including the dreaded morning drinking, and was on my way to alcoholism. I was pretty drunk that first time with my landlord, so, I bent over and took it for the five minutes it lasted." Hanna started to laugh ironically.

"That's some seriously dark humor, Hanna."

"That's because I am dark, Jack. Or at least that's what I had become," Hanna said forcefully. "That's the point. I'm definitely no saint. I'll be honest, Jack, by that time, I could be bought. If someone would have offered me enough money, I would have allowed that someone to do a lot of things to me. That's why I let my landlord have me and why he thought that he could come back with his friend for another go-around. Thinking back to then, and once I was near eviction, sitting on my couch with a bottle of wine in my hand, I wasn't even using a glass, I wished I would have turned around when my boss told me I was going to lose my job and I knew how that sex party was going to devolve but I would have gone back. While I was drinking alone on my couch, I wished that I hadn't walked out of the party. I seriously regretted it. I knew that everyone at that party was going to have a turn with me, probably more than one at a time and I still would have gone back. I would have done anything they wanted with the men or the women and I knew that my future was going to be filled with the same kind of sex. It was what he was into. I picked up the phone to call the asshole. I was ready to beg and was going to ask him to give me a second chance and agree to do whatever he wanted, whenever he wanted, and with whoever he wanted, but I couldn't complete the call. So, I dropped the phone on the couch. I am admitting to you that I had become that person. That's something that was hard to admit to myself. But I'll tell you what, I like myself better and homeless and here than I have for a lot of my life. I'm at the very bottom, as low as I can go, but I'm curiously free of who I was before and I don't feel any anger. It's almost as if that part of my life didn't happen. I rarely even think about it or what I might have done if given a second chance. I'm not interested in revenge in the least and I haven't even felt the desire to drink. Not that you can get a drink here."

"Okay, I get it, but you are seriously fucked-up."

Hanna laughed out loud, "Ya think!?"

"Geez, Hanna," Jack said, shaking his head.

"Actually, Jack, I was hoping to attach the past tense to your "I'm fucked-up" statement. But, until you get your head out of your ass and get brutally honest with yourself, you can't improve or move on. I'm not doing anything but taking responsibility for my own shortcomings and I'm letting all that other stuff in my past go away. All those people are dead to me. They don't matter. I'm honestly in a kind of peaceful place in my head right now."

"I'm glad for that. I'm sorry for what you went through, though."

"Thanks," she said quietly. "I do appreciate that."

She snuggled back against Jack's body and pushed his hand firmly against her breast and held it there. They were both quiet for a few minutes.

Jack then said, "I guess neither of us are model citizens."

Hanna chuckled and they lay quietly and cuddled.

Sometime later, Jack interrupted the quiet and said, "I really hate to say this, Hanna, but you need to go. The cameras are going to come on in a half an hour. I don't think I want people to put us together as a couple. I'm not sure if that's unavoidable, though. I need to think. I'll walk you to your train and see you home."

"I might want to jump your bones again."

"Geez, Hanna. I'm not sure that I can keep up with you."

"Ah, getting old? That's alright. I'll just go home and take care of my own needs in front of the cameras for whoever is watching. First, I'll take off all of my clothes facing the cameras so that they will get a good view. Then I'll let my hands roam my flesh. What do you think of that picture, Jack? Then I'll..."

"Okay," Jack blurted, feeling the immediate return of his arousal. "We have a few more minutes before you need to go." He pushed her to her back, kissed her lips, and they moved together in a desperate embrace.

"God, I've missed you, Hanna," Jack whispered.

Twenty minutes later, they were both dressed and stepping out of Jack's room. They took the train not speaking much and lost in their own thoughts. They exited the train and he walked her to her door.

She asked, "Will I see you again, Jack? Did I reveal too much tonight?"

"Like I said before, Hanna, I fell in love with you all those years ago. I think you know that. I think it's why you felt free enough to completely level with me." Then Jack cocked his head and asked, "You did completely level with me, didn't you?"

"Yes, Jack. And for what it's worth to you, I've never stopped loving you either."

Hanna pulled his face to her and kissed him for a long time. They separated and she sighed, looked deep into his eyes, turned, and opened her door. "Don't be a stranger, Jack. I think I can skip the peep show for the guys on the cameras now and sleep."

She half-smiled, walked in, and closed the door.

He turned and walked away.

Chapter 23

Homeless City

9:00 am the next morning, Jack Morgan was to check-in at his new job at the warehouse. It was the last interview with the supervisor to make sure that the supervisor wanted to hire him. They didn't want people who were going to be a liability or get hurt on the job. Jack had stressed his computer skills to his social worker who put those skills at the top of her recommendations.

When Jack walked in, Micky, the supervisor, was agitated. Most of the work on the floor had come to a screeching halt and pallets were backing up as workers waited for the okay to continue bringing in the merchandise.

Jack approached Micky, "Hi, Mister Micky. I'm John Black. I spoke to you last week about a job and I believe my social worker sent over my paperwork."

Micky didn't look up. "Damn it, I don't have time for this right now. Wait over there." Micky was poking at a computer pad and swearing under his breath. "I hate fucking computers!"

"Maybe I can help," Jack offered.

"You help? How?"

"I'm good with computers."

Mickey breathed out sharply. He said, “What was your name again?”

“John Black.”

“I don’t know what’s wrong? Every time I make an entry, it takes five minutes for it to allow the next entry. At this rate, a decade is going to pass before we get today’s loads checked-in.”

“Huh? So, your system just slowed down today?”

“Yeah, today is the worst, though we’ve had days when the system was a little slow, but not like this. It did seem that the system had been getting a bit slower, maybe because of all the stuff that we’re receiving, but this is ridiculous.”

“You should take me to your main computer. I could see what’s slowing down the processes.”

Micky glanced up as if seeing Jack for the first time. “Okay?”

“Good, let’s check it out.”

Micky handed the computer pad he was holding to his receiving clerk and said, “Keep trying,” then to Jack, “This way.”

He led Jack to the office where they first met.

“Just a minute. Let me log in.”

Jack stood in front of Micky’s desk and pressed at his index finger to try to record Mickey’s password while Micky one finger poked it in. It wasn’t a sure thing that Jack would be able to record it. Sometimes it worked and sometimes it didn’t, depending on the system, the distance, and any other impediments.

Micky asked, “What do you want me to do now?”

“Are you on your start-up screen?”

“Yep.”

“Let me at your computer.”

Micky glanced at Jack suspiciously but shrugged and stood.

Jack sat down in Micky's seat and looked at the screen while Micky watched over Jack's shoulder.

Jack typed a command then waited. The task manager screen popped up and Jack scrolled down the list of processes. "Okay, boss-man. You got a few things happening at the same time that's slowing your system. The first thing is a system update. The update is dragging probably because of this second thing. Someone from outside is monitoring everything arriving in your warehouse today. Is there anything important arriving that's maybe out of the ordinary, something that someone would want to flag?"

"No one told me?"

"Huh? Do you want me to speed up your system?"

"Yeah, If you can?"

"I can. I'll postpone your system update until 7:00 tonight. That will help a lot. As for who is monitoring your deliveries from the outside, I could lock them out but they would probably get back in pretty fast. Depending on who they are in the chain of command, they would figure out that I locked them out from here. They would think it was you and would probably rip you a new asshole."

Micky laughed, "Maybe skip that step."

"Good call. There are a few more things I could do to speed things up incrementally. Separately they aren't much but together it should help." Jack typed a few more commands then said, "Okay. Go ask your receiver if things are close to normal."

Micky nodded and walked out of the office.

Jack worried about who was monitoring the system. He temporarily locked the person out, then deleted the short piece of coding that he had hacked into the system the day before that was designed to slow it. He then gave himself a backdoor password into the system from this location and made himself an administrator. He wouldn't necessarily need Micky's password now unless he wanted to do something and make it look like it was Micky. He swept away all clues about what he had done then let the person monitoring back in and thought more deeply about who might be spying from the outside. That was a real concern and it seemed odd but he didn't fully know what was going on in this strange city. It could be normal. He was going to need to be more careful when he hacked. If he had time, he could figure out who was spying but today wasn't the day for that.

When Micky returned to his office, Jack was leaning back in Mickey's chair.

"Better, Boss?"

"Yep. All better."

"Good. Now about that job?"

"What was your name again?"

"John Black."

Micky shuffled through a stack of papers on his desk, "Ah, here it is." He lifted John Black's paperwork that had come from the social worker and glanced through the lines of type. He looked back up at Jack and said, "I need an early receiving clerk. You come at 4:00 am and you're off by 3:00 pm."

"Sounds good to me."

"How much training are you going to need?"

"Not much. I worked for a grocery chain before I became homeless," Jack lied. "I worked to receive product in that job. I'm sure it isn't much different."

“Great. I’ll need you tomorrow. I’m already down one of my morning receivers who left sick a couple of days ago. Come in at 4:00 am and I’ll hook you up with Steve for some training. He’ll be glad to see you. He’s needed to work a couple of extra-long shifts because we’re short of help.”

“Great,” Jack said as he signed off the computer.

Micky said, “I’ll see you around 7:00. That’s when I come in.”

Jack nodded and turned for the door. That went well, he thought as he walked from the warehouse. Then, I wonder what Hanna’s up to?

Chapter 24

Langley Virginia

CGSS Headquarters

Edward Chang rose from his desk and walked into Atwood Colter's office.

"Mister Colter, the vaccine has arrived and has been checked-in."

"Thanks, Edward."

"A weird thing, though, and it might be nothing but it seemed that I was locked out of the system for around fifteen seconds. It might have just been a glitch. Also, for some reason, their systems were moving extremely slow that day. Again, it was probably nothing, and maybe related to why I seemed to have been locked out, but I thought I would mention it."

"Thanks," Colter said, dismissing Edward but Colter was always suspicious.

As Edward was exiting the office, Colter said, "Edward."

Edward returned.

"Go back and continue to monitor that location. Report to me anything out of the ordinary."

"Will do."

Edward turned and left the office. Colter picked up his phone and contacted Adam Cruz, the President's

Chief of Staff, and informed him of the growing epidemic at Homeless City and suggested that he contact the head of the CDC instructing him to use the vaccine on the residents.

***

Cruz then picked up his phone and dialed Doctor Jacob Lasater, the head of the CDC, "Hello, Jacob, I understand that we have some kind of a flu outbreak in Homeless City."

Lasater responded, "I hadn't heard that?"

"It was just reported to me. I think we should start inoculating the population there. You should contact Doctor Haines at HC."

"I don't know if there is enough vaccine there to vaccinate the entire population."

"If not, we should send more. The president cares deeply and is very involved with the wellbeing of the residents of Homeless City."

"I understand. I'll immediately contact Doctor Haines in the city."

"Thank you, Jacob. I'll tell the President that you are on it."

"Yes, Sir, right away."

***

Lasater hung up and quickly called Doctor Haines at Homeless City. The last thing he wanted was to delay if Fergusson wanted something done.

"Hello, Doctor Haines. Doctor Lasater here."

"Hello, Doctor Lasater. To what do I owe this pleasure?"

"I have heard that you have an outbreak of some kind of flu in your city."

"That's true. We are handling it, so far, but I'm becoming worried."

"Do you have enough flu vaccine to inoculate your population?"

"Not sure, but we're also not sure if it's the flu."

"What else might it be?"

"I don't know, yet."

"So, do you need more vaccine?"

"Probably not. Yesterday, we received a full shipment of the vaccine. It's being distributed to the various infirmaries as we speak."

"That's great. I'm glad to hear that you are on top of this problem. The President wouldn't want anything negative to happen with the residents there. I'll tell him that you are beginning to inoculate the population, just in case."

"We can begin inoculating our residents at the rehab facility and the Asylum tomorrow and the other residents a few days later. I'm afraid though, that we are going to need more ventilators. We are nearing our max."

"I will have additional ventilators sent ASAP."

"Thank you, Doctor."

"Good. I'll report your response to the President. Thanks."

***

Lasater called back the Chief of Staff Cruz who called Colter.

“Mister Colter, I’ve spoken to Lasater of the CDC who just reported to me that they will begin inoculating the residents tomorrow.”

“Thank you, Adam. Keep me informed.”

***

Colter hung up and shook his head. He had no bout of conscience where administering this fake flu vaccine was concerned, his troubled thinking was because he knew that if the American population ever found out about this, he and Fergusson and others wouldn’t just be locked up for it, they’d be executed. It would be important to keep the circle of people who knew about this as small as possible. Some might even need to meet with accidents.

Part 4

Z Plague...

Chapter 25

Homeless City

Eastern Medical Facility

Doctor Charles Linder stepped out of the small makeshift emergency room that had been set up at the front door of the Eastern infirmary. He needed a break. This emergency room was no more than a tent that allowed the nurses and doctors to triage the flood of incoming patients that began a few days earlier in Homeless City.

Doctor Linder removed his mask and gloves and wiped his face. One of the nurses, Brook Coleman, stepped out also.

"Geez," she said. "What's going on here?"

"Don't know. This is some kind of epidemic. I just got off the phone with Doctor Haines who talked to Doctor Lasater from the CDC and he told me that there has been a small outbreak similar in Long Beach, but nowhere else in the country that he knows of. They don't want it to spread in case it's dangerous."

"Dangerous? Oh, it's dangerous."

"Yeah."

"And it seems to be spreading."

"I've sent specimens out to the closest labs but haven't heard anything back yet. They told me that they should have an answer for the sickness by tomorrow. It's tough to treat a sickness if you don't know what you're fighting, and now we're out of ventilators."

"So, we can't send some of these patients out?"

"Doctor Haines told me no. He said that Lasater told him that came directly from the President's office. He told me that we'll have to do the best we can. He also told me that some flu vaccine has arrived and is being distributed to the Asylum and rehab patients first because they are the most compromised, then it will come to the other medical facilities in the city. We'll need to get the population here inoculated as soon as possible if the vaccine is to work. It may already be too late."

Coleman nodded then asked, "Do you think this is a flu?"

"I do. It's acting like some of the severe forms out there."

"Well, I hope they get the vaccine to us sooner rather than later. It couldn't hurt."

Linder nodded and put back on his mask.

Several people walked up to the tent coughing.

Linder took a deep breath, stood, and walked back into the tent followed by Coleman.

Chapter 26

Langley, Virginia

CGSS Headquarters

Atwood Colter waited for word from his computer specialist that the vaccine had been distributed.

Edward Chang walked into Colter's office and announced, "Sir, that shipment that you were waiting to hear about has been distributed to the various places in HC."

"Thank you," Colter replied shortly.

"There is also a report that the sickness that's going around is spreading throughout the population and the construction workers in the city. I understand that they are beginning to inoculate people at the Asylum today."

"Thanks," Colter replied.

Edward nodded and left Colter's office.

Colter shook his head and wished that Fergusson had not made the decision to proceed with this mass murder now that it was beginning. Not known for having much of a conscience, guilt began making an appearance in Colter's usual amoral thought processes.

Chapter 27

Homeless City, California

Jack Morgan waited outside the library for Hanna to get off of work. He could see the lights go out in the back of the library as the employees mingled and gathered at the front of the building. The double doors slid open and the employees all walked out together then began walking as a group towards the underground trains. Jack caught up with the group.

"Hanna."

She stopped and turned around.

"Hi," he said.

"Hi, Jack."

"Are you busy tonight?"

"Oh yes. First, I need to rush home and shower, then put on my ball gown for the dance at the prince's palace."

"Well, I'm not sure that I can top that evening. I guess I should let you get to your big dance, Cinderella."

"Okay, so my story wasn't so original."

"I happen to know of a place where we can have some privacy."

"You are no prince, Jack, but I guess I'm no Cinderella either."

Jack smiled and Hanna walked to him and briefly kissed his lips.

"Let's go," she said, taking his hand.

They walked to the trains and sat together. As the train departed, Hanna said, "Jack, I'm worried about Trish. She hasn't come back to work and hasn't returned to her apartment."

"I can possibly check on her. I can't guarantee that I'll find her but I might be able to. What's her last name?"

"Richards, Patricia Richards."

"Okay. When I go to work in the morning, and can get alone with a computer, I'll see what I can find out."

"Thanks, Jack."

They proceeded to Jack's apartment and began undressing as the door swung shut.

Chapter 28

Homeless City

The next morning, at 3:30 am, Jack's alarm went off. He shook his head and rubbed his face. Hanna had stayed past midnight and used him more than once. He wasn't complaining but he was lacking sleep. It was worth it, though, he thought as he scraped himself from bed.

He dressed and hustled to the train that took him to the warehouse where he worked. He could use a cup of coffee but that would need to wait until his first break.

When he entered, he was five minutes early. Steve was standing at the time clock and he raised the injected device planted in his upper arm to be scanned to begin his day. Jack did the same.

Steve said, "Geez, John, did you get any sleep last night? You look like shit."

"Not much. I couldn't sleep for some reason. I'll be fine."

They walked to the loading docks and took over for the two receivers whose shifts had ended. This being only one of two receiving docks for the entire city, there was a never-ending stream of goods and supplies arriving daily and nightly.

They both got to work checking in the freight and making sure it was properly directed.

Two hours into his shift, Jack asked, "Hey, Steve, mind if I take a break? I could use a quick cup of coffee."

"Nope. Go ahead. See you in ten minutes."

Jack logged off of his computer pad and walked towards the breakroom. The breakroom was down a dim hallway that led to two large restrooms, both men's and women's, past his boss's office, and to a large breakroom with tables, chairs, and an automatic coffee machine.

When Jack passed Micky's office, he waved his hand over the door entry security pad and the door popped open. He knew that he had little time. He quickly closed the door and sat at Micky's desk. The computer had been left on but he needed to get past the sign-in screen. He signed in as administrator 1211 then began searching for Trish.

He typed "Patricia Richards" into a field marked search. A picture of Trish came up with her file and identification number. At the bottom of the screen, there was a box labeled, "*locate.*" He hit the button. Trish's little green box with her number came up in the Asylum. It was not moving. She was probably asleep in bed. Where she was located was displayed: "The infirmary."

He clicked on her numbered icon and it directed him to an ICU bed deep in the bowels of the Asylum on the underground fifth floor. He found Trish on a ventilator and watched as she received a shot. She didn't move as she received it. She didn't look well. He panned the camera back and could see rows of beds no more than three feet apart, all filled with patients. All seemed extremely sick.

Jack left Trish's bedside then opened a program that allowed him to access the cameras everywhere on the hospital floor of the Asylum. He popped in and out of rooms where doctors and nurses were working to help patients. He saw everything from lifesaving procedures to sponge baths. No one he saw looked to be in good shape. Some had their sheets pulled over their faces. They didn't make it.

Jack glanced at the clock, seven minutes had passed, so he logged off and wiped the computer clean of his intrusion. He had temporarily turned off the cameras and wiped off his image from the time he entered the office until he had left. The cameras came on just as he stepped towards the breakroom. He grabbed a quick cup of coffee, added a bit of cold water to cool it, gulped it fast, then headed back to work.

Chapter 29

Abandoned Military Base

Outside Homeless City

Brian McKinsey woke disoriented. He was a construction worker who lived in the old abandoned military base outside Homeless City. It was still dark outside; the sun would soon be up.

He could feel that he had a high fever and was having trouble breathing and trouble thinking straight. The room where he slept always smelled of unwashed workers and dirt but this morning, it smelled of human waste and maybe death.

He tried to blink away the approach of delirium and confusion and forced himself up on his elbows.

"Hey, Phil," Brian said loudly.

His friend, Phil, didn't appear to be breathing.

"Phil! Wake up. I'm sick. You okay?"

There was no response from Phil's cot that was no more than four feet away.

Something was very wrong in this large communal sleeping space.

Brian forced himself to sit on the side of his cot. The room swam around him. He closed his eyes and rubbed his face with both hands. When he opened his eyes, the entire dimly lit room was no more than a blur. He pushed himself up to an unsteady standing position and shuffled over to his friend's cot.

"Hey, Phil."

Again, no response.

Brian shook his friend's shoulder.

"Dude. You need to wake up."

Nothing.

Brian pulled back Phil's covers and gasped, "Damn!"

Phil's mouth hung lifeless and his eyes were unevenly open. His skin appeared grey and mottled.

"Help," Brian called weakly.

Others in the room were already stirring from the beginning of Brian's commotion. Some were not moving in their cots. The smell of Phil having soiled himself wafted from the covers and lingered ominously in the air around his cot.

"Jesus," Brian said quietly and he crossed himself, glancing at his decease friend, not believing that he was gone. He pulled the covers over Phil's head.

Brian remembered Phil becoming worse the day before and now, Phil had passed. He shook his head.

Everyone in the room was beginning to get up. The quiet room now had the sounds of rustling but nearly no one spoke.

Brian stepped back to his cot and sat disbelieving as others checked on their friends and several walked over to look at Phil.

Horacio Gonzales pulled back Phil's covers and said, "Aye Dios Mio. He's dead." He recovered Phil's face.

Horacio walked away.

Several people said that others had passed in the night. It seemed that everyone in the room was in a state of shock.

One man said, "Someone, go get the boss."

The blankets shrouding Phil moved slightly. Brian glanced at the blanket a little surprised but he knew that people did move sometimes after their deaths.

Phil sat up!

"Phil?"

Phil turned further and stared at Brian like he was prey. His eyes had lightened but were not yet white and the skin everywhere on Phil's body was mottled as if the blood couldn't reach every part. Wearing boxer shorts and a tank tee-shirt, Phil draped his bare feet over the bed and onto the floor. He moved his mouth as if trying to speak but nothing but unintelligible grunts, gurgles, and growls came out of purple lips. It was as if he had forgotten how to speak.

Men in the room began to take notice of the risen Phil. They stepped back as if they might catch some contagious disease.

Brian said, "Damn, Phil, I thought you were dead. You should get back into bed. You don't look well."

Brian got up to help his friend back into bed. He glanced around and every person who had been thought of being dead was doing the same thing as Phil. All were rising. There must have been more than a dozen. Some had gotten to their feet and looked shaky and confused.

Brian reached Phil and began to speak, "They gonna be surprised that you're—"

Those were Brian's last words. Phil jumped on Brian and bit down on his upper arm ripping a huge piece of deltoid flesh. It hung in a sheet. Brian screamed. Then Phil bit into Brian's neck silencing him. Blood spurted from his carotid artery.

The others who had risen from the dead also began attacking anyone who had the misfortune of being too close. As the attack continued, all of the rising dead were feeding on their coworkers. They ripped gaping hunks of flesh from the bodies of those who were sick and hadn't died, but in the midst of the attacks, the risen dead would suddenly stop feeding as those who had been bitten began to change into whatever the risen dead had become. No one was able to escape as the attack was swift and savage. Soon, everyone left in the room was either dead or changed. These changed creatures then began to feed on those who died but hadn't changed. It seemed that most of the too sick workers lying in their beds were nearly devoured before they could change. Others with massive wounds seemed to have no pain and the profuse bleeding slowed then stopped even with ruined flesh hanging in tatters from the wounds.

These now blood-soaked creatures all turned and walked from the barracks where the construction workers had slept and headed out towards the construction site. When one of the foremen, Hal Stewart, pulled up in his jeep, the things from the barracks ran towards him. He had stepped from the jeep and hadn't noticed the attack. When he turned and saw these escapees from a nightmare heading his way, he jumped into the jeep and tried to drive away but the group caught him and began feeding. Stewart died quickly and was eaten in the front seat of his jeep leaving only blood-soaked bones and entrails.

Chapter 30

Homeless City

Death Valley, California

The first deaths from the mold hit Homeless City just as the first injections of the lethal vaccine began being administered to the homeless who had been taken to the Asylum and the Rehab Center. In the first two days, more than fifty thousand doses of the vaccine had been administered. The news of the deaths spread quickly through the residents of Homeless City by word of mouth and overhearing, but no official word that people had died from the sickness had been forthcoming. The faux flu vaccine was continuing to be administered through the Asylum and Rehab Center and would soon move to the population at large.

Jack Morgan met Hanna at the library the next evening.

"Hi, Jack," she said, seeing him approach.

He half smiled and took her aside from her library coworkers. "I found Trish. They have her on a ventilator. She isn't doing well. I didn't have time to poke around much. I'm going to need to find a computer that will give me more time."

Tears had gathered in Hanna's eyes. She shook her head. "Poor Trish."

"I'm sorry, Hanna. I'll try to get more information. They were giving everyone in that ward shots of some kind, maybe the vaccine."

"Maybe that will help."

"Maybe. But there's something that I don't understand about this big vaccine shipment that the city received. It had to have been shipped before anyone was sick. To me, it doesn't make a lot of sense but it could just be something that works for a lot of different diseases. I'm sure that, in general, the homeless aren't very healthy and maybe it was forward planning but I can't help a feeling niggling in the back of my mind. It's a sense that I always listen to and it's saved my ass more than a few times."

"What now?"

"I'm going to go to a place where I had used a computer before. It's an office that is closed until morning. I'll have more time to poke around without being discovered."

"When are you going?"

"Right now. I'll walk you home then go."

Hanna nodded and they turned for the trains.

Jack walked Hanna to her apartment then caught a train towards an office that had a computer that he had already breached. The office was near the induction building that was now dark with no new homeless having arrived tonight.

Jack waved his hand over the door lock pad and the door clicked open. He walked quickly into the office not turning on the lights then to a computer in the back of the dark room. He felt for the USB port and slipped his flash drive into the port. He then turned on the computer and when it came up to the start screen, it asked for his password.

Jack glanced towards the front of the building to make sure that no one was walking by the windows. He typed in his password then went to his special account to see what the intelligence community was up to.

He spent some time poking around the fringes of some of the people that he knew were involved with looking for him. There was nothing new there. It seemed that they had hit another dead end in the Netherlands.

Jack smiled. "Sorry, guys."

He tapped into Atwood Colter's private messages.

"Huh?" he whispered out loud.

Colter had a few messages with someone named Feinberg about the vaccine shipment to HC.

Homeless City?

Something about a labeling change? Or problem? Or something? The exact words were, "We were able to fix the labels."

"Fix the labels? What the hell?"

Feinberg reported back that everything went smoothly.

"Okay?"

Something isn't right and who's Feinberg?

Jack moved away from Colter and back to the Asylum to check on Trish. He pulled up the cameras and went directly to her ward and she seemed to be sleeping comfortably. He got into her chart and could see that she was deteriorating. They had given her a few different shots and intravenous treatments but nothing seemed to help. He could see that, at least right now, her vital signs were stable enough.

Jack panned back and could see the entire ward. Several people had their sheets pulled over their heads. Jack shook his head. They didn't make it.

He pulled up a file that listed the people who had died from the sickness. Most had already been taken to the morgue. Jack was in full intuition mode now and he pulled up the camera feeds at the morgue. Several coroners were working on bodies on the stainless-steel tables. The bodies were all in various stages of their autopsies. Some with their chests and abdomens open.

He was about to leave when, out of the corner of his eye, he saw movement from one of the bodies. That seemed a little strange, but not unheard of. The body was of a tall man, African American, and without question, dead. The head seemed to turn towards the coroner and the eyes opened. The coroner pushed the head back to where it was and closed the eyes.

"Weird," Jack whispered.

He closed the program, wiped the computer of any record of his visit, reset the cameras, and removed his image. He walked to the front of the office and glanced out of the windows to make sure that no one was outside. He then slipped out of the door and walked quickly to the train platform nearby.

Chapter 31

Long Beach, California

Long Beach is a bustling community of approximately 500,000 people. The first deaths of those exposed to the mold began soon after their exposure when a bus accident near the construction site sent a dozen people to the emergency room and ten more to the morgue.

The emergency rooms in the city were already beginning to overflow with patients that were having trouble breathing because of an adverse reaction to the odd mold that seemed to be spreading inland. Patches were showing up near waterways and drainage ditches.

City Morgue

Long Beach, California

Scratching, then scratching again... Low scratching... Muffled...

Long Beach's Coroner David Meltzer turned his head.

Mice?

Not a good thing in here, he thought.

He took off his wire-rimmed glasses and cleaned the lenses with a tissue then went back to his clipboard and checked the notes that had arrived with the last stiff. A man lay on a gurney in a body bag in his forties who died after walking out in front of a bus...

Dumb ass...

Meltzer read the notes. Most of the bones in the guy's body were broken or cracked. Severe internal injuries... Open skull... Brain matter outside of the cranium...

More scratching...

Meltzer looked up then glanced back down at a corpse on his stainless-steel table, a woman he was working on who died mysteriously in her sixties. He had her chest opened and had taken some samples for toxicology. The results should be back shortly. In examining her organs, he thought she shouldn't be dead. Heart good... other organs normal, even above average. She was found in her home by a relative. Only been dead for a few hours before her discovery. There had been a respiratory illness that had recently sprung up in Long Beach making a lot of people sick and overwhelming some of the emergency rooms. He thought that this may have been the reason for the woman's demise. Toxicology might find something. Could be some kind of virus or bacteria.

"Odd," he thought aloud.

Stitch her up and move on to the next one... Bagged and tagged... "Into the freezer, Ma'am."

Scratching...

"What—is— that?"

He turned his ear to try to figure out the direction of the noise.

Finishing with the woman, Meltzer slid her back into her freezer compartment.

A bang as if something metallic was struck. It sounded as though it came from one of the freezer compartments.

Meltzer walked over to the bank of stacked cabinets. There was some kind of movement in compartment A6. He raised his eyes and thought it might be postmortem muscle contraction. He slid open the compartment. The compartment was low and he had to bend down to peer inside. A hand reached out and grasped his throat. It was cat-quick and it gripped like a vise. He struggled then blackness filled his vision from the edges...

The next morning, a call came into the Long Beach police department for a missing person, Doctor David Meltzer. It was from his wife. He was the coroner who worked the late shift at the morgue. The wife had repeatedly tried to call her husband on his cell phone. The police asked how long overdue he was and she said around three hours and that it wasn't like him. Officer Darrel Harper said that they don't begin a missing person's report until the person has been gone for 24 hours but in this case, he has a car close by and he will have the officer check the morgue. Thank you was her response.

***

When officer Anna Ramirez and Officer Jimmy Olsten arrived, they walked into the morgue's lobby and it was obvious that something was wrong. Ramirez and Olsten both pulled their firearms and sighted down their barrels as they slowly walked further.

Ramirez called using her two-way radio, “We got a situation here.”

Harper at the station asked, “What’s the situation, Ramirez?”

“This place is a mess. We’re walking through now and there is blood tracked everywhere, no bodies, though. I don’t get it. We’re entering the autopsy room now. There’s an unattended body on one of the tables. Chest fully opened and organs in containers. It appears as though something had taken bites off of the deceased person on the table. There are hunks of flesh missing from her arms and legs. This place smells like death.”

Ramirez stepped around the autopsy table and froze. She said into her com, “Found a body. There’s a man in a white lab coat lying on the floor. His head is nearly severed from his body and most of the skin has been ripped from his face... Jesus.”

Ramirez shuddered then continued, “Several of the lockers are open and what looks like smoke is rising from the lockers. Looks like refrigeration. I’m going to take a look. The floor in here is full of blood. I guess from the guy on the floor. His head is attached to his body by just a small piece of skin... What’s that?”

Something had moved in the shadows of the room.

Officer Olsten replied, “A person?”

A man with no clothes ran from a dark corner and attacked Olsten who had walked away from Ramirez. The man’s skin was bone white and had visible gaping wounds. Ramirez fired her weapon striking the nude man but he didn’t seem phased. He jumped upon her partner and bit his neck, quickly severing his carotid artery. This man was inhumanly fast and strong. Her partner fell. The man turned towards Ramirez. She fired again striking the man's chest but the man whose mouth was filled with a hunk of skin taken from the neck of her partner turned and ran at her. She moved behind the table where the autopsied woman laid and put the table between herself and the attacker. The attacker began to climb over the table.

She shouted into her com, "We need backup here. Olsten is down!"

The attacker paused and seemed temporarily confused. He turned back as if to go back to Ramirez's fallen partner when Ramirez raised her gun and fired at her attacker at point-blank range, striking him on the side of his head and blowing away half of his skull. The attacker dropped.

She glanced over at her partner who could not be still alive. The blood had fountained from his neck. He had been laying in the growing puddle but then he slowly began to rise.

The naked man who had lost a good portion of his head began to push up as if attempting to also rise but he fell back to the floor.

Olsten was now standing with slumped shoulders facing away from Ramirez. He looked wobbly and his arms dangled at his sides. His shoulder was covered with the blood from his neck.

The naked man pushed up again as Olsten turned and stepped around him. Olsten walked towards Ramirez.

"Get over here, Olsten!" Ramirez shouted, fearing that Olsten would be attacked again.

The naked man had pushed himself to his knees and looked as though he would stand. Ramirez fired her gun again and struck the naked man in what was left of his head removing most of the rest of it and he fell to the floor. His fingers moved as if wanting to grasp something.

Both of Ramirez's arms were extended as she kept her gun pointed at the now headless man on the floor. A slight haze from firing her weapon lingered in the air and the smell of gunpowder mixed with death and the coppery smell of blood.

She glanced at her approaching partner and noticed that Olsten's eyes were now nearly white. The next thing she knew was that Olsten was upon her. She struggled with Olsten as he attempted to bite her neck. She tried to push him away but he was inhumanly strong. She shoved her forearm under his neck, temporarily causing him to stumble. Her arm slipped up and he bit the arm causing a deep wound. Ramirez screamed and shoved the barrel of her gun under her partner's chin and pulled the trigger. The bullet entered Olsten under his chin and exited through the top of his skull. He dropped to his knees, then fell to the floor.

Ramirez holstered her gun and covered her arm with her hand, then felt something in her veins as if someone had injected her with snake venom. She began to shutter and shake as if she had gripped a fallen high-power line...

Chapter 32

Any place where the mold spores touched, it began to grow. It appeared in small patches and seemed to love the environment of Southern California. It spread on the wind and on migrating bird flocks. Tiny patches of the mold soon appeared in Nevada, Arizona, New Mexico, south of the border in Tijuana, and as far east as El Paso, and Juarez.

As it landed, it slowly grew and then within a day began producing spores that would again be carried on the wind.

At the same time, the mold appeared in tiny patches in Northern California, Oregon, Washington, and western Canada. Everywhere the mold appeared, people began to cough.

Chapter 33

Oval Office

Washington D.C.

President Fergusson sat behind his desk waiting for Colter to arrive. The door opened and Colter walked in and stood before Fergusson.

"Mister President. The vaccine has been administered to the entire Asylum and the Rehab Center population. It is now, as we speak, being administered to every sick person that crosses into any infirmary. This sickness that has spread around Homeless City has been a timely coincidence and has provided us with a good excuse to inoculate the entire population. We have had several people try to escape the city recently. I'm worried that we may be understaffed to keep a mass exodus prevented from the city. I think we should send some reinforcements for the Citizen Guard now deployed."

"That's all good news, Atwood. Really, what do I care if they all leave after they have received the vaccine? That might even be a better plan than to keep them all there to die."

Colter thought about that for a second. He truly hadn't considered that. He half-smiled. "You might be right. Maybe we should reduce the Citizen Guard and make it easier for people in the general population to leave if they want to. It would give them up to a couple of weeks to die somewhere else. If people in the city become afraid of the sickness, they might begin trying to leave in mass."

"Let's pull most of the Guard out of the city. That will leave just enough to make it seem as though nothing has changed but will give people the green light to run if they desire. We might even consider bussing people from the city as the infection increases."

"That's even better. Might be a good time to set up that tent city you wanted. We could begin transporting people there within a couple of weeks."

Fergusson nodded then said, "I'll get together with Cruz to go to Congress for the funding."

The next morning, before the sun rose, troop carriers started out of the city loaded with Citizen Guard.

Chapter 34

Homeless City

Hanna stood behind the desk checking out books for the patrons of the library. The morning had been quiet with few people entering.

A woman approached with her two-book limit and Hanna smiled. She scanned the woman's arm to identify her, then scanned the books. Hanna smiled and handed the books back to the woman and said, "Have a nice day."

The woman coughed, smiled back, and walked away and out of the double doors.

Ann Voss, the head librarian, stepped up to the several people working the check-out desk and said, "Tomorrow, our entire staff will be inoculated for the flu that's going around. A healthcare nurse will arrive at noon with our vaccines."

The workers behind the check-out desk all nodded and went back to helping patrons.

9:00 pm and Hanna walked from the library having finished for the day. A familiar man joined her as she walked.

"Hi," Jack Morgan said, keeping pace with her.

"Hello, Jack. Haven't seen you for a couple of days?"

“Been busy.”

“Glad to see you now.”

“Me too.”

They walked together and caught the train home.

Jack said, “My place or yours?”

“Your stop is closer.”

“My place then.”

Hanna nodded.

Jack asked, “How was the job today?”

“The library was slow. I think because so many people are sick. I’ve had a bit of downtime there so I’ve been looking for some good books to read.”

“Let me know what you find. I could use a good book.”

Hanna nodded again then said, “We’re all getting vaccinated tomorrow for the flu. Supposedly, a nurse is bringing the vaccine to the library.”

“Huh? Sounds like they’re going out of their way to inoculate everyone.”

“Well, a lot of people are sick?”

Jack nodded then said, “Here’s my stop.”

The train stopped and they both stepped out and walked together towards Jack's room.

Chapter 35

Homeless City

Early the next morning and on his break, Jack stood outside the warehouse as the sun was rising. He was suspicious and the details behind this vaccine kept niggling at him and wouldn't let him alone. Who was this Feinberg guy? And what was up with the relabeling of the vaccine? Why would someone want to relabel a vaccine?

He stared into the distance, lost in thought. Nothing in this city seemed right. It wasn't a real city, though, he admitted to himself. It was a contrived city to handle the problem of homelessness so it didn't rise out of nothing and grow organically the way most cities began. And that might be part of the oddness.

The day was going to be warm. The skies were clear and the sun was just about to rise over a mountain ridge to the east.

A noise of rumbling from down the main boulevard caught his attention. He straightened and watched as troop transports in a column rolled down the street, heading out of the city. These transport vehicles were filled with Citizen Guards. Were they bugging out or just out for training? A column of a dozen motorcycled guards finished the parade from the rear.

"Huh?" he thought aloud. Then, "Strange?"

His break over, Jack walked back inside and began working to check in loads at the receiving dock. His trained mind was working in hyperdrive as he tried to make sense of the things he was noticing. Nothing was adding up. Maybe they were reducing the Guards because the city was now secured. Maybe they had anticipated more trouble that didn't materialize. And what was up with the vaccine and Feinberg?

On his last break, Jack slipped into Micky's office when Micky left for his lunch. It was 11:30 and he would only get a few minutes with the computer.

Jack slipped his flash drive into Micky's computer and once his sign-on screen popped up, he logged in and began searching the web for this guy Feinberg. He found several Feinbergs but only one was interesting. Dale Feinberg, former Central Intelligence agent specializing in Bio-warfare.

"What the hell?"

Jack left the web and signed onto his private and secret account. He typed, "Dale Feinberg."

Dale Feinberg: CIA twenty years... Biowarfare analyst and researcher... Fort Detrick, Fredrick, Maryland... Now in private research...

Jack dug deeper... Still receiving government checks?

"Huh? That's strange?"

Correspondences: A full list... People associated with his job at a biotech company called BioFuture. Nothing unusual...

Here... Three emails to Atwood Colter.

The first message was not in response to another email. It just said, "Can do." Must have been in response to a phone call.

The second message, two days later, "Proceeding."

"Proceeding with what?" Jack whispered.

The third message, two days after that, "Completed and shipped."

"Huh?"

There must be some record of the receiving and shipping of a pallet of vaccine? He found BioFuture's corporate website and easily hacked into its record section. He began checking several possible dates for a large shipment of vaccine from somewhere.

Time was passing and Jack was becoming nervous. His boss might be back shortly.

"There it is," Jack whispered aloud.

A shipment from Fort Detrick to the BioFuture warehouse. One million doses of vaccine? Fort Detrick doesn't produce vaccines. It produces death.

"What the hell?"

Then shipped out three days later.

Five more minutes...

Jack left the BioFuture website and hacked into the city's administrator Archer's account. He searched the email and found a directive directly from Colter to pull nearly all of the Citizen Guards from the city.

Another head-scratcher... Why?

A disturbing thought leaped into Jack's mind. Is something wrong with the vaccine? No, they wouldn't do that. Not even Colter would pull something like that... But would Fergusson?

He logged off the computer, pulled his flash drive, and scrubbed his tracks, then he stood and walked from the office. He turned down the hallway just as Micky entered heading back to his office.

"Hey," Jack said as he passed.

"Hello, John."

Jack continued past Micky and a sudden fear struck him. The tendrils of it invaded his veins leaving an odd chill that settled in the pit of his stomach.

"Shit!" he said to himself. "Hanna."

When he was near a door to the street, he turned, opened it, and jogged away from the warehouse. Something is wrong with the vaccine, he thought. Nothing else makes sense.

He began to sprint towards the library. When he reached it, there was a sign on the door that stated, "Library closed for one hour. Will reopen at 1:00."

He glanced in the windows and could see a line of people in the very back of the large room between the shelves of books. Why were they lined up?

He waved his hand over the electronic door lock and it popped open. He walked quickly and could see that people were getting shots. The line approached a couple of nurses and those library employees in front rolled up their sleeves. Then after an alcohol swab, the nurses injected them and they rolled their sleeves back down and walked off. Hanna was just reaching the front of the line.

Jack walked up and smiled at the nurse. He firmly took Hanna's arm and pulled her from the line. She glanced at him as though he had lost his mind.

He whispered, "We need to leave right now."

The nurse said, “This vaccine isn’t optional.”

“Let’s go, Hanna.”

“What’s wrong?” Hanna asked, now confused.

The nurse spoke into a communication device, “We have a code 10 at the library.”

“Let’s go,” Jack said forcefully. Then he whispered so no one else could hear, “I think there’s something wrong with the vaccine.”

Hanna looked into his eyes for some deceit. She knew that he had found something.

They began to head out of the door. Four Citizen Guards with automatic weapons stepped in and leveled their weapons at Jack and Hanna.

All of the library personnel stared with eyes wide and mouths agape.

The Citizen Guards didn’t ask any questions to Jack or Hanna but one guard asked the nurse who had followed them to the door, “Is this your 10s?”

She responded, “Yes.”

“Cuff them.”

Both Jack and Hanna were cuffed and pushed into the back seat of a black SUV which pulled out rapidly.

Hanna glanced at Jack questioningly.

His expression was grave and he leaned up to look out of the front windshield.

No one spoke. The guards were silent.

Jack thought that he probably could have overpowered the four guards but Hanna might have been shot so he hoped to find another way out.

The SUV continued down the main boulevard and turned onto the side street that gave access to the Asylum. The tall, chain-linked fence gate opened and the SUV pulled into the Asylum’s grounds.

The SUV parked, the guards climbed out, and one opened the two back doors, and gruffly said, “Get out.”

One guard was holding his automatic weapon. The other was not.

They lead Jack and Hanna into an unmarked building and past a thick glass window with another guard watching. There was the sound of door locks clicking, then Jack was taken through one door on the right of the window, and Hanna was taken to the left, through another. The doors closed securely behind them.

Chapter 36

The Asylum

Homeless City

Once separated from Jack, Hanna was taken to an elevator, which descended to the second floor. She was then taken to some kind of holding cell. She sat alone on a plastic chair and waited.

No less than two minutes later, a man and a woman, both in Citizen Guard uniforms and with bad attitudes, stepped into the small room where Hanna was being kept.

The woman commanded, “Stand up.”

Hanna stood.

The woman scanned Hanna’s arm then said, “Place both hands on the wall and spread your legs.”

Hanna complied.

The woman patted Hanna down and checked her pockets.

The woman then said, “Open your mouth.” She checked to make sure that Hanna wasn’t hiding anything there.

The woman barked, “Now, Ms. Scott, why were you and the other man leaving the library in such a hurry and why did you not take the vaccine?”

Hanna didn't know what to say. She just stared at the woman.

"Well?" the woman asked.

Hanna finally said, "I didn't want the shot. Some vaccines make me sick."

"That's not an excuse here. Who is the man you were with?"

"Just a guy I met here."

"What's his name?"

"Jack, um, I mean, John. John Black."

"You said, Jack."

"I think he said that was his nickname."

"What's your relationship with him?"

"Friends, I guess."

"Friends? Are you and he in a sexual relationship?"

"Um, well, we've become close."

"That's evasive. Are you having sex with him, or not?"

"That's impolite."

"Answer the question, please."

Hanna breathed out, "I suppose."

"We will have a look at the recordings of your room and his to know for sure, so you might as well not lie to me."

"I understand."

"Did you know him before arriving at Homeless City?"

"Nope."

"Again, Ms. Scott, we have ways of verifying the truth, so I suggest that you do not lie."

"I understand."

"So, you did not know him before you arrived?"

"No."

The woman stood and said, “You will be kept in this Asylum until we are sure that you can be trusted. You will be taken to a room and given an Asylum gown. There you will wait as we check out your story. Do you understand?”

“Yes.”

The woman pulled Hanna to standing and ushered her out of the room. The two Citizen Guards walked Hanna down the hall and to another room. After leaving the elevator, they walked Hanna down a corridor. People could be heard screaming and shouting from some of the rooms. The rooms all had a large window in each door. Some of the people were gazing out of the window into the corridor while others were laying on their beds. They all were in what appeared to be hospital gowns with no shoes or socks.

When the woman and male guard reached an empty room with Hanna, the woman scanned the door lock and it popped open. She pushed Hanna into the room. The male guard took off Hanna’s handcuffs and stood back. Hanna rubbed her wrists.

The woman said, “Take off your clothes and put on this gown. Do it now. We can’t leave until we have your clothes.”

Hanna stripped down to her underclothes and stood.

The woman said, “Everything. Hurry up.”

Hanna had spent so much time naked upon her arrival that it no longer seemed to matter to her. She complied. Once her underclothes were off, she handed them to the woman and stood with her arms crossed over her chest.

The woman handed Hanna her gown and she pulled it on as the man looked on. The woman searched Hanna's pockets. Finding nothing, the woman gave Hanna a derisive look, left the room with the male guard, and shut the door. It locked with an audible click.

Hanna breathed out, sat on the bed, and looked around. The floor was cold on her now bare feet.

She softly said, "What is going on here?"

Chapter 37

The Asylum

Homeless City

Upon arriving at the Asylum, Jack had been ushered into an elevator by the guard. Two other guards stood in the elevator, both with automatic weapons. The three guards who now stood with Jack were silent and aggressive and they held their weapons on him. One guard pressed the button to floor 5. The bottom floor was 6. Next to the 6 was a label that read, "morgue."

The elevator began to rapidly descend and Jack could see as each floor passed. The elevator stopped then the doors opened into a hallway painted white with soft lighting. There were cameras in various places on the ceilings to watch the elevator, any place there was a door, and places where a new corridor branched off from the hallway that Jack had stepped into.

No one spoke.

They reached a holding cell deep in the bowels of the Asylum. Being five stories underground, there were no windows. The cell was small with a bench. They pushed Jack inside and closed the door. It locked with a click.

Jack stood and listened at the door, waiting for the guards to leave. When they did, he waved his hand over the exit pad and the door lock clicked open. He half-smiled, relocked it, and sat down. He took his flash drive out of his pocket and slipped it into his shoe.

Ten minutes later, two guards in Citizen Guard uniforms opened the door. One had a handgun and the other a taser.

"Get up," the man with the taser barked.

Jack nodded.

They patted him down, checking his pockets, then walked him to another unmarked room down the corridor. When the door was opened, there was a man in a Citizen Guard uniform sitting at a table.

"Sit," the guard barked.

Across the table from the man was an empty chair. Jack sat.

The man had a Lieutenant's bar on his shoulder. He was young, no more than twenty-five with crewcut dark brown hair and a scar above his right eye, causing a part in his eyebrow.

He glanced at Jack with cruel eyes.

Jack stared back unblinking.

The two guards remained in the room.

"Name?" the officer asked. He raised a scanner to Jack's arm. It beeped and then he glanced down at a computer pad.

"John Black," Jack replied.

"Not Jack?" the officer asked with some skepticism.

"I've been called that, but it's not my given name. I've been called other things not so pleasant also. Do you want those names too?" Jack responded sarcastically.

The officer was on a short fuse. His face reddened. He put both hands on the desk and pushed himself up to tower above the seated Jack. The move was to intimidate but again Jack didn't blink.

"Are we going to have a problem?" the officer asked.

"I don't know, are we?"

The Lieutenant became angrier.

Jack breathed out, "What do you want to know?"

"We've reviewed the video feed from the library and we want to know why you pulled Hanna Scott from the line? Why did you leave your job in such a hurry and run to the library? Why did you not want her to have the vaccine?"

"The lady and I have a relationship. She told me that some vaccines in the past had made her sick. When I overheard someone saying that everyone was going to get the vaccine at some of the workplaces today, I remembered what she told me and jogged to the library. I didn't care if I got the vaccine. I was just thinking of her."

That explanation even sounded lame to Jack's ears. He had been thinking of an excuse but hadn't come up with anything even remotely plausible. If he were doing the interrogation, he wouldn't believe his story. In his business, though, the questioning would, at this point, become much more painful. He didn't think that they would be that motivated in this setting.

Then Jack asked, "What's the big deal? You can have a few people not get the vaccine and it will still be effective."

"I don't see in your file that you're some kind of doctor."

Jack didn't comment.

"So, John, you and the lady are in a sexual relationship?"

"Yes."

The officer breathed out then said, "You will be taken to a room, strip-searched, and given a gown. You will remain in this institution until we have checked out your story. Take him away."

Jack was going to need to make his move to escape. Time was running out.

An odd knock came at the door. It didn't sound so much like a knock as it sounded like a bump. Just then alarms rang out with the rhythmic thrum of warning.

The officer glanced away from Jack. He looked confused.

More bumping at the door and it sounded like on the walls also.

Jack turned to look towards the door.

The officer glanced at the guard closest to the door and jerked his head. "See what's going on out there."

The guard removed his sidearm, unlocked the door with the pad, and cracked it open. Gunshots rang out in the corridor. The door pushed in violently and the guard fell backward. People with a strange appearance pushed through the now open door. There were at least a dozen, maybe a few more. Most were in Asylum gowns but some were naked both male and female. One was in a Citizen Guard uniform. They all looked wrong. Their expressions were somewhat blank. Their faces all had an odd pale-grey look. Most of their mouths dripped with blood and their eyes were nearly white.

The people fell upon the guard who had stumbled back and began biting him. He screamed.

Jack jumped over the desk to put it between himself and the people entering.

The officer and remaining guard pulled their firearms and began shooting at the people entering the room but it had little effect and just seemed to rile the intruders.

The alarm continued to ring in the background and shots continued in the corridor. People screamed. It was chaos.

The officer's eyes were filled with fear. He seemed to have forgotten about Jack and had back-peddled to the wall but now was frozen. He continued to pull the trigger of his gun, though it was out of bullets. The officer watched as the second guard was overwhelmed. The first guard had been bitten so savagely that his face was reduced to ragged flesh hanging from bone.

Jack stared at the group of people entering. He recognized Trish. She was in an Asylum gown, the front of which was blood-soaked. Her eyes were empty and white.

The throng moved towards the officer as the first guard rose now not seeming to be interesting to the odd mob and he turned and walked towards the officer who was frozen with fear standing against the back wall. This guard's eyes had lightened and were nearly as white as those entering.

Still handcuffed, Jack turned the table on its edge and placed it between himself and the mob, more of which had entered the room. He ducked behind the table and slid it to the right as the mob moved left, towards the officer. The mob, at that moment, didn't seem interested in Jack.

The second guard was rising now with hunks of flesh hanging in patches. Jack stood behind the table and slid it towards the corner of the room. The mob moved around him and had reached the officer. The officer tried to fight them off but they easily overwhelmed him and he disappeared behind their flailing arms and tattered, blood-soaked gowns. The floor was slick with blood.

Jack reached down and lifted the guard's handgun that lay in a puddle of the guard's own blood. One of the mob, a nude man, turned to see Jack lift the gun and moved quickly at him.

Jack hoped that the gun wasn't empty, but it might not help anyway as the previously shot individuals in the mob had not seemed harmed by being shot before.

The man opened his mouth wide and barked an odd squawk. Jack shot him between the eyes. The man dropped like a stone.

Jack slid the table closer to the door and pushed it at several of the mob who noticed him. They pushed the table aside just as Jack slipped out of the room, pulling the door closed. He quickly turned to see if he might be attacked. There was carnage everywhere Jack looked and no one was on their feet in the hallway. He waved his hand and locked the door. The mob pressed against the closed door but couldn't exit.

Jack looked closer at the people laying in the corridor. Several guards lay nearly completely eaten, their heads off their bodies. There were also people from the mob laying with terrible head wounds. They clumsily tried to push up to stand as if attempting to retrain their devastatingly injured brains.

Jack checked the gun he was holding to find that it was now empty of shells. He had used the last one. He dropped the gun then quickly gathered several others he could find, tucking them into his belt. He then rifled the guard's pockets for anything he could use. He found handcuff keys and unlocked his cuffs and dropped them to the floor. He pulled the belts off of the two headless guards. These belts had tasers, bullets, and several clips filled with shells for the hand-guns.

For the first time since the mob's attack into the room, Jack had a second to think. His mind began to process everything at lightspeed that had occurred. First, the dead were not staying dead. Why? That didn't make sense. He saw one of the guards who was with him in the interrogation room with terrible injuries rise. He should have been dead or at least, writhing in pain. Next, he considered the other attackers. Some of them had injuries but not many. They had the appearance of someone already dead. Did they come from the morgue? He glanced down at a nude woman whose arms and legs were moving but her head injury was massive. Jack glanced at her foot. A toe-tag. At some point, this woman had died. She was probably in a freezer. That's why she had no clothes... He shook his head. Trish, he thought with some anguish. He felt guilty for leaving her in the room but she was one of the assailants, not someone being attacked.

Jack checked to see how many rounds were left in the gun he was holding, five rounds. He popped the clip back into the gun.

"Hanna! Shit!" Jack thought aloud in sudden panic, his voice echoing in the hall.

Two Citizen Guards ran from around a corner at Jack. They were white-eyed and had their arms extended. Jack fired five shots rapidly and struck each rushing guard several times in their heads and they temporarily dropped. One began to rise but Jack didn't want to waste a round on him. Jack put the empty gun in his belt and grabbed another. He checked to see that the clip was full. He pulled several loaded clips from the two guards he had just shot, jammed them in his pockets, then sprinted to an elevator, but he didn't push the button. He was afraid of what might come out of the elevator doors. Instead, he found a stairwell, cautiously opened the door, and peeked inside, sighting down the barrel of his handgun. There was blood but no bodies. A red light pulsated with the insistent alarm.

Stepping in, he shut the door behind him. He definitely wasn't going down so he quietly started up. He wanted to run but was afraid that he might be attacked by something unsuspected, maybe even a Citizen Guard.

The alarm continued its loud, unrelenting, pulsating ring accompanied by the flashing red strobe.

He stepped cautiously upward, sighting down the barrel of his gun to the next floor and the blood tracks that filled each step seemed to lead out of the door on this landing. He passed that door and stepped upward to the next floor. Here, there was no blood. He carefully opened the door to the third floor. He knew that finding Hanna in this huge place was like finding a needle in a haystack. He needed to get to a computer.

As he opened the door onto the third floor, he could see an office. Two Citizen Guards were gathering up items and both ran from the office and to an elevator. Jack waited... The alarms continued... He watched as the elevator door closed then he sprinted into the office and closed the door behind him. He placed his pistol on the desk by a keyboard and hit a key. The sign-on screen appeared.

A citizen guard burst into the office. He barked, “Who are you? Get your hands up!”

Jack lifted his gun and fired, hitting the Guard in the throat. The Citizen Guard dropped.

Jack put his gun back down and began frantically typing, searching for Hanna Scott.

Hanna’s picture appeared on the screen with her identification number. He hit the “*locate*” button. Second floor. Room 2276. He pulled up the camera feed in the room and Hanna was sitting on her bed in a gown and looking around. The red light from the alarm pulsated in her room through the windowed door.

He stood then, took off the clothes of the guard on the ground, and pulled him further inside the room. He stripped out of his grey jumpsuit and put on the Citizen Guard uniform. The fit was snug but it would do. There was blood on the collar and down the front of the jacket. Jack clipped on the gun belt and sat back down in the chair in front of the computer.

He logged off the computer then paused as he had a thought. He logged back in as administrator and shut down all the cameras in Homeless City, every one of them. Then he unlocked all the doors in the Asylum and all the doors in the rehab portion of the city. He knew it would be impossible to help all of the people but if he opened the doors, at least they would have a chance to run. He then cut off all the computer systems from the outside world. No one from the outside would be able to get into the city's computers, at least not for a while.

He logged off and walked out of the door to get Hanna.

Chapter 38

CGSS Headquarters

Langley, Virginia

Edward Chang rushed into Atwood Colter's office.

"Sir, something has gone very wrong in Homeless City!"

Colter glanced up from something he was reading as he sat at his desk. "Slow down, Edward." Colter knew that people were going to start to die because of the switched vaccine. He figured that was the problem. "What's up?"

Edward was breathing hard. "There's been some kind of uprising in the city. I was able to see people attacking guards. It doesn't make sense. It seemed to start in the Asylum's morgue and at the Rehab's morgue."

"Show me."

Chang sat at Colter's computer and pulled up the camera feeds from both morgues. Nothing. The feeds were no longer operational.

"Huh?" Chang said questioningly, then, "I have a copy on my computer."

He typed a command connecting his computer with Colter's. "Here, look at this."

Colter peered into the monitor. What he saw chilled him. It appeared that people came from the shadows and attacked people working there. After they attacked the people working in the morgue, the people who were attacked seemed to join the assailants, standing up and following the attackers out of the room and down the hallways where they attacked anyone in the halls. Some of their wounds were ghastly.

Colter was nearly speechless as he watched with mouth agape then the recording went black. "Why did the cameras go out?"

"I don't know. We don't store much here. All the storage servers are in the city by your orders. We get feeds and I captured this one while I was watching it. Then, as you saw, everything went black. Someone either shut them down or there was some kind of catastrophic failure."

"So, there isn't anything coming out of the city right now?"

"Let me check..." Chang punched the keys then said, "No. Nothing."

"Go and try to get back into their systems."

"Yes, Sir."

Chang left Colter's office and Colter sat back in thought. He had purposely wanted everything recorded at Homeless City to be kept there in case it needed to be destroyed... What was going on there? He rubbed his face.

Colter reached for his phone and called Edwards Air Force Base. He contacted General Hodges.

"General, I need a flyover of Homeless City in Death Valley. I need you to send drones. I have to know what's going on there."

"I can have them there in half an hour."

"Do it. Contact me when they arrive."

Hodges rang-off and Colter sat back in his chair. He thought, could these people have found out that they were being given a drug that would kill them? But they were acting so savagely. Could the drug have caused some kind of psychosis? He would wait to contact President Fergusson until he had more information.

Chapter 39

The Asylum

In the hallway, the lights were dim and the alarm blared with red lights strobing the walls floor, and ceiling. It was like a nightmare impossible to wake from.

Jack made sure that the three guns that he possessed were fully loaded. He tucked one into his belt behind his back, kept one in the holster on the gun belt he was wearing, and kept one in hand. He slung the two additional belts with ammo over his head and under his arms, crisscrossed over his chest then walked away looking for some way off of this floor.

The floor was deserted. The alarm rang and it seemed that everyone took the warning and vacated.

He stepped quickly past the elevator and back to the stairwell. He thought about taking the elevator but he feared that it would open into a swarm of the people who seemed to be... What? Changed?

He had to get to Hanna.

He entered the stairwell and walked into several of these changed humans. They instantly recognized that he was there and started for him. All of these people had startling wounds as if they had been in severe car accidents. Flesh hung in places through ripped, blood-soaked Asylum gowns. Why weren't these people writhing in pain? How could they still be alive?

Jack shot at the creatures striking their heads and they fell onto the stairs and it seemed that they couldn't rise though they tried.

The shots seemed to wake up a group of creatures in the stairwell below. They rushed upward, their feet slapping the steel stairsteps. Some growled while others squawked. The coppery smell of blood and the scent of flesh beginning to putrefy wafted up from the lower portions of the Asylum.

Jack would add more gunpowder to the smell. He began firing at the heads of the coming hoard as he backed up towards the next landing. As they fell, their fellows stepped over and onto the fallen bodies. Some of those who had been shot attempted to rise but others lay still.

One gun emptied, Jack reached behind to his belt and pulled his second gun. The hoard continued up the stairs. 9 more shots and Jack finally reached the landing to the second floor. He tucked his emptied second gun away and pulled his third. He opened the door with no less than twenty of these things now following as more had joined the chase.

Jack stepped onto the second floor, sweeping his gun from left to right. No assailants. He shut the door, swiping his hand across the pad and locking it. The floors below must have housed male prisoners because most of those in the stairwell were male and in gowns or naked. He quickly reloaded his guns, ejecting the spent clips and jamming new clips back in. It wouldn't do any good to find Hanna if he couldn't defend them.

As he began to look for room 2276, he glanced into the rooms through the windows. The doors he could see on this floor were unlocked but the women had not tried to leave even though the alarm droned on. The alarm was starting to get to Jack. It was loud and unnerving.

Jack thought about warning these women but he didn't know why the people in this place were going crazy. He was afraid that he would need to fight them. He passed a room where a woman was up against the window, her face, hands, and gowned body were pressed to look out. She watched Jack pass but made no attempt to communicate with him.

Jack proceeded past. He glanced at room number 2217. He had further to go. He continued to sight down the barrel of his gun not wanting to shoot someone innocent but also not wanting to be attacked.

A woman streaked from around the corner. She was barefoot in a gown and unquestioningly panicked. She froze when she found herself looking down the barrel of Jack's gun. He was close to squeezing the trigger.

She held her hands out. "Please, don't shoot me! Please!" She began to weep.

Jack lowered his gun and waved her over. He said, "I have to get to a friend. You can stay with me but if you decide to leave, don't take the stairs. It's full of danger."

"Can I stay with you?"

"Yes."

Jack proceeded forward with the woman close behind.

Jack said, "Keep a look behind us. If you see anyone, let me know."

The woman nodded.

Jack glanced up to see room 2260 and across the hall 2261. Hanna's room should be close now.

They came to a corner and Jack peeked around it. There, a man was in a gown taking bites out of a woman lying on the ground. She was also dressed in a gown. He was ripping mouthfuls of flesh and gown from the woman, pulling and twisting, tearing gown to get to skin. She had been struggling the moment before but she soon went limp.

Jack quietly stepped around the corner and found Hanna's room. He slowly crept towards it trying to not make a sound.

When they had come close, Jack said to the woman with him, "She should be in there. Open the door and go inside."

Jack didn't enter, though. He approached the man who was eating ravenously and shot him in the head. He dropped. Jack observed the woman on the ground. Most of her gown had been chewed off and ragged flesh hung in puddling blood.

Jack turned back to Hanna's room but the woman hadn't entered. She stood in shock from watching the man eating the gowned woman.

"What's going on?" she whimpered between tears. She was shaking. "What's happening here?" The woman was losing it.

"I don't know," Jack responded and it was the truth. He had no idea.

"Look out!" the woman with Jack shouted.

Jack turned to see that the woman who was being consumed by the man had risen and was walking at Jack. She was picking up speed, moving quickly, and dripping blood from severed veins and destroyed flesh. The front of her body was completely unrecognizable as being human. Most of her flesh had been ripped from her face and the front of her body. She looked like she'd been turned inside out. Her lipless mouth opened wide.

Jack fired two quick shots into the woman's head and she dropped. He moved to Hanna's door, and wasted no time, quickly pulling it open. Hanna had heard the shots and cowered in the corner of the room.

"Hanna! Come quick," Jack commanded.

Hanna's head had been lowered between her knees. She slowly glanced up and said, "Jack? Is that you? Jack?"

"Now, Hanna! Come now!"

Hanna rose from the corner and stepped quickly to Jack and the woman with him. Jack glanced at both. They were in flimsy hospital gowns with obviously nothing underneath and no shoes. They wouldn't be nimble. He would have to remember that.

"We got to get out of here, Hanna."

Hanna nodded spasmodically.

The other woman stood nearly paralyzed with fear. She shook.

Jack barked, "Let's go!"

He stepped quickly to the elevator. He had no choice. The stairwell was out. He pushed the button. They stepped in and he closed the door. Once inside, he reloaded each spent clip. He had few loose shells.

"Do either of you know how to shoot?" he asked.

They both shook their heads no.

"Okay, here's the problem," he remarked as he finished loading an empty clip and slipping it back into the belt. "You've both seen what we're facing.

When this elevator stops, those things might be out there. If so, we need to close these doors as fast as possible. Hanna, stand by the button. Push it if you see anything that scares you. Understand?"

She nodded.

The elevator stopped on the first floor and the doors began to slide open. Gunshots rang out and a Citizen Guard standing in front of the elevator doors was firing at something unseen.

Hanna pushed the button to close the doors but the guard's shoulder hit the nearly closed doors and they started to reopen.

Jack grabbed the guy's shoulder and pulled him inside the elevator. The guy fell backward and landed at Jack, Hanna, and the other woman's feet. The elevator doors closed as arms reached to get inside.

The guard looked up blinking. He saw that Jack was holding a gun on him but he said, "What the fuck, man? What's going on out there?"

Jack lowered his gun, took the guard's arm, and raised him to his feet. He glanced over the guard to make sure he didn't have any wounds from the creatures. Jack was quickly beginning to get a picture of how this sickness that turns people into these creatures occurs.

Jack said, "I'm John. Do you know how we can get out of here? Is there roof access from the top of this elevator shaft?"

"Yeah, I think so."

Jack stared at the ceiling for a few seconds then said, "Okay, good. Hoist me up."

The guy locked his fingers and lifted Jack to the faux ceiling. Jack pushed up a ceiling tile and looked at the situation above the elevator. There was a place to stand and a ladder leading to a door above.

Jack said, "This looks good. Pass the ladies up and I'll pull you up."

The guard nodded and said to Hanna, "You first."

She nodded and he locked his fingers and hoisted her up. Jack pulled her through and she stood on a wide landing that surrounded the elevator ceiling.

"Now you," the guard said to the other woman. He lifted her also to Jack. Jack pulled her up.

Jack looked down and said, "It's solid on this edge. Can you jump and reach it then pull yourself up?"

The guy wasn't very fit. He had a paunch in front and was breathing hard. He tried to jump but could only get his fingertips on the edge.

"I can't make it."

Jack nodded. "Just a minute." He turned to the two women and said, "Start climbing the ladder."

They nodded and started up. The woman went first, then Hanna.

Jack snickered and said, "We're going to need to find you guys some clothes later."

Hanna glanced down and could see Jack's view. Then glanced up and got an eyeful of the woman above. She breathed out and resumed climbing.

Jack then jumped back down into the elevator and said, "I'll hoist you up. I can climb out myself. Don't start up the ladder until I get up."

The guy nodded.

Jack jumped down and the guy said, "You're not a Citizen Guard."

"No," Jack replied, "I took this coat off of a dead guard because it was thick and I saw that people were being bitten. I thought it might protect me some."

The guy glanced at Jack suspiciously, then at the blood-soaked collar and shoulder of the jacket. He nodded and said, "Let's get the fuck out of here."

Jack hoisted the guard up, jumped, and caught the edge, then pulled himself up.

The women were at the top of the ladder. Jack looked up and said, "Come down a couple of rungs. I'll climb up and try to open the door to the roof."

The two women both came down a few rungs and Jack quickly shimmied up. When he reached the women, he climbed around them and to the door. He pulled the latch, but it was locked, so he waved a hand over the locking mechanism, and it unlocked. He carefully pushed open the hatch door and peered out. No one was on the roof.

"We're good," Jack said, fully opening the door hatch and climbing out. He helped both women out then the following Citizen Guard.

When the guard was out Jack said, "We need to get out of this city. Something has gone very wrong here."

The Guard said, "We're close to the place where we keep our vehicles, but most are gone with the guards who left."

"Yeah? What's up with that?"

"Don't know. They told us that we were going to be on a skeleton crew, that the guards were needed elsewhere."

"Well," Jack said. "Let's hope we can find something to get us out of here."

Jack walked around the roof. It was a flat terrace with four-foot cement sides that looked down to the streets below.

Jack walked to one wall and peered down followed by the other three. There was chaos in the streets in front of the Asylum and the Rehab Center in the near distance. Several people in gowns were attacking other people in gowns. Citizen guards were shooting at people in gowns killing innocent people who hadn't changed into whatever they were changing into. They lay dead in growing puddles of blood. There were a few guards who had been bitten and were now attacking other guards. It was clear that the number of creatures was growing.

The guard who was with Jack also looked down and said, "Damn! I don't understand?"

Jack said, "It looks like the majority of trouble is coming from the Rehab Center and the Asylum. Maybe we can circle behind the residences and get out of town."

"There are roads that encircle the city. We could give them a try but there is only one way in and one way out by the Induction Center. Another thing, all communications are down in the city. No one can communicate with anyone so we can't coordinate a response to what's happening. Everyone is on their own."

Jack nodded then said, "This side of the building appears to be safe for now. Let's crawl down the fire ladder here and run to the place where the vehicles are kept. I'll go first, then you," Jack said to the guard, "Then you two."

Everyone nodded and Jack started down.

The top of the building was a little less than two stories high so the climb down was quick. When Jack hit the ground, he swept his gun left and right. As the guard neared the ground, five people in gowns with white eyes ran shoulder to shoulder around the corner. They were fast and they sprinted clumsily at

Jack. He raised his gun and shot. The first one dropped. He fired again and the second dropped. By the time he was ready to fire the third time, the three were upon him. He kicked the first to reach him, a man in a tattered blood-soaked gown, knocking him to the side and sending him sprawling. He shot the next one leaving just two. The man who he kicked was up and coming fast. Jack swung a backhand and struck another man who was closest knocking him to the ground then he fired at the one who had just gotten up and hit him between the eyes. Jack turned then and shot the fifth person, a woman with white eyes and nearly no skin on her face. She dropped in a heap.

The guard had watched the precision of Jack's response to the attack from his perch on the ladder as he was descending. There was no wasted motion, no panic or fear, just efficient mayhem.

He came down the rest of the way and said, "Damn! You military?"

"Used to be." Jack turned and watched the women coming down the ladder. "Quickly," he ordered.

The women reached the ground. Hanna was under control, cool, sharp, and focused but the other woman seemed semi-frozen in fear.

Jack said, "We need to move."

They started off to the left. They needed to get through the gate on the backside of the Asylum, then cross the street just one building away from the motor bay. The woman did not follow.

Hanna turned and stepped back to the woman. "What's your name?"

"Dawn."

"Dawn, listen, we need to move. I'll stay with you. Give me your hand."

The woman reached out her hand. Her eyes were filled with tears. Hanna took the woman's hand and started out, pulling her gently.

The four jogged along the wall of the Asylum and to the back gate. It was unattended.

"No one's here?" the guard remarked questioningly. Then he said, "Strange?"

Jack approached the gate and pushed it open. The group walked from the Asylum grounds.

They all moved together in what could only be described as an alley. Here the buildings were closer together than on the wide boulevard in front of the Asylum. There were doors on the buildings to the right all marked with numbers and nothing else and the Asylum wall on the left.

Jack asked, "How much further to the vehicles?"

"Just around the corner to the right. There's a driveway that leads into the building. I'm sure the bay doors are closed. It's designed with a place in the middle to service the vehicles and parking around the service bays. If we needed to get the vehicles out rapidly, all the bay doors could be opened but for day-to-day use, we just used the driveway."

They slowed as they reached the corner. Jack peeked around. There was no one in sight. They glanced behind and no one followed.

Hanna crouched and rubbed her bare foot, it was bleeding. Jack glanced at her.

"Listen, Hanna. I think what's happening here is some kind of contagion. I'm not sure if you need to be bitten or if just coming in contact with these things can infect you. You need to avoid blood until we can get you some clothes and shoes."

She nodded then ripped a portion of the bottom of her gown and wrapped both feet tying them with a knot on top. She helped Dawn do the same.

Jack started forward and reached the driveway into where the vehicles were kept. The driveway was long, sloped upward, and curved to the left. As he walked, he listened for any sound that might give him a clue as to what awaited them at the top of the driveway. There was no sound. By this time, he would have expected to hear something.

They reached the top of the driveway and Jack peeked around the corner. The lights were dim as if the facility was closed down for the night. Jack's eyes widened. Standing in places around the motor pool were changed people. They stood almost still, swaying slightly, their arms hanging limply at their sides. They looked at nothing. Their chins were lifted as if trying to smell the air. Their mouths were slightly opened and their heads oddly moved left and right as if attempting to pick up sounds of prey. Few were in gowns. Most were dressed in mechanics overalls and Citizen Guard uniforms. All had gaping wounds. Jack counted twenty. They were spread evenly around the several vehicles that remained and the service bays.

Jack signaled for everyone to stop. He turned and joined his group and nodded for them to leave. Jack, Hanna, Dawn, and the Citizen Guard quickly and quietly moved back down the driveway.

When they reached the bottom, Jack said, "It's filled with creatures. I counted twenty that I could see. They were just standing there as if waiting for something. It's the damnedest thing that I've ever seen. I don't get it."

Dawn began to weep and shake again.

Jack asked the guard, "What's the next building?"

"Guard barracks."

"Let's go there. Is there an armory in the barracks?"

"No. It's in the next building."

"Maybe we can get some clothes and shoes for the ladies," Jack said, nodding at the two women.

They moved down the street and to a back door to the barracks. Jack again took the lead and approached the door. Hanna was behind him, followed by Dawn, then the guard.

Jack tried the door handle but it was locked. He waved his hand over the entry pad and the door unlocked with a click. He carefully pushed the door open and stepped inside, sighting down the barrel of his pistol. The three waited outside.

Behind him was a rush of sound. He grabbed Hanna's hand and pulled her to him. A group of more than a dozen creatures rushed by the door, tackling the guard and Dawn. They tumbled in a mass of bodies, bloody and tattered clothing, and flailing limbs. One of the creatures hit the door frame but fell outside.

"Noooo!" Hanna screamed.

Dawn and the guard tried to get free but teeth and claws bit and scraped.

Jack forcefully slammed the door shut and he and Hanna fell to sitting with their backs pressed against it. There was pounding on the door from outside.

"No, Jack. We need to help them."

"It's too late, Hanna. Once you're bitten, it's too late. I've seen people change in less than thirty seconds. Dawn and the guard are with them now or dead."

Hanna stared at Jack confused.

Sadly, Jack said, "I never learned the guard's name."

Two figures appeared in silhouette in the dark barracks just outlined by a dim light from behind them. Jack had his gun pointed. The figures quickly moved in Jack and Hanna's direction. Jack fired his pistol twice. The figures' heads bucked backward and dropped.

"Are you sure they were bad?" Hanna asked in a near whimper. She was becoming unglued.

"Yes. It's something in the way they hold themselves, an odd posture."

"Shit," she whispered. "What is this? What's going on?"

"Some kind of hell. Come on, Hanna. Pull it together. I need you to focus."

She nodded but wasn't coping. Her eyes were filled with tears.

Jack stood and waved his hand over a control pad to turn on the lights. When the lights came on, three more of the creatures dressed in Citizen Guard uniforms were heading straight for them. Jack emptied his pistol dropping all three.

He handed it to Hanna and ordered, "Reload this with a clip."

She nodded, wiped her eyes with her arm, and took the gun. "What do I do?"

"Pop the clip out by pressing here." He pointed, then push the new clip inside the gun."

"Got it," she said, steeling herself.

Jack had his second pistol ready and sighted the room. He glanced down at the two silhouettes that he had first shot and they were also creatures in gowns. He noticed that there was no bleeding from the head wounds and he wondered at that. Before the creatures were changed, they bled just the same as any human but soon after, they changed and were shot, they no longer seemed to bleed. Why? It was like their blood coagulated in their veins.

He started forward with Hanna behind. Beds lined both sides of the room and lockers stood between each bed. All the beds were made and their covers neatly and tightly tucked.

"Check the lockers for clothes for you."

Hanna walked between the beds and pulled open the lockers. All were empty.

"Shit," she said. "Nothing."

Jack lowered his gun and walked back to the dead creatures in Citizen Guard uniforms. One was a woman. He contemplated having Hanna use her clothes. He was afraid, though, that Hanna might be infected by whatever was infecting everyone. He looked at the dead thing's shoes, pulled one off, and there were no bodily fluids anywhere on or in the shoe. He pulled off the second and it was also clean.

"Put these on for now and we'll find you some clothes later. I don't think you can use her clothes. I'm afraid you might become infected."

Hanna reluctantly nodded, took off the makeshift foot-wraps, and pulled on the shoes. They were Citizen Guard lace-up boots, black with steel toes. She stood in her flimsy, sweat-soaked gown, the bottom of which was ripped up to her upper thighs. Her skin was visible through the wet gown as if she were in a wet tee-shirt contest. Her face was dirt and tear-streaked and her light brown hair was stringy and wet with sweat. Wearing the army boots, she stood with her toes pointed inward.

Jack glanced at Hanna with an odd expression.

She stared back then said, "Soooo, how do I look?" She grinned and held her arms out as if displaying herself in a prom dress. "Stylish, don't you think?"

"Geez, Hanna, you truly have the darkest sense of humor."

She grinned broadly.

Jack said, "Let's find another way out of here."

Hanna nodded then her smile turned to grief. "Dawn, Jack. Poor Dawn."

Jack looked down and sadly nodded. "Let's get out of here."

A thought leaped into Hanna's mind. She blurted, "Trish? What about Trish? We need to go back for her."

Jack's expression turned back to sadness, "She's changed, Hanna. I saw her in a room. Her eyes were white."

"No," Hanna whispered and she began to weep again, barely able to get the words out, "Are you sure?"

"I'm positive."

Hanna put both hands over her face. Her shoulders shook as she convulsed in her grief as if losing her only child.

Jack approached her and took her into his arms. "I'm sorry," he whispered into her ear.

She hugged him tightly and said, "How can this be happening?"

He gently pushed her back and looked directly into her eyes and said, “We need to get out of here, Hanna. I think everyone in this city will eventually be changed. I don’t see any way to stop whatever is happening here. We don’t have time for grief. Not now. If we don’t leave, that will be our fate.”

She nodded spasmodically.

Jack separated himself from her and led her to the other side of the building. He cracked the door and peeked out. To the left was open desert visible through a chain-linked fence. To the right was a road that appeared to wrap around the outside of the city. There was no one in sight.

Jack cautiously stepped outside. He took two steps and waved Hanna out. The sun was dipping towards the horizon to the west. They began to the right.

Jack said, “It looks like this road skirts the outside of the city. Maybe we can find some kind of vehicle.”

“Can’t we just run?”

Jack could feel the sun beating down on his shoulders. The late afternoon was becoming extremely hot.

“I don’t think so. We’re surrounded by brutal desert. We might be able to make it but I doubt it. Let’s see if we can find a car or motorcycle or something.”

Hanna nodded.

They continued forward and Jack noticed an odd shadow cross his path. He glanced up. A sleek drone passed overhead. He quickly turned his head to the ground.

Hanna saw his odd reaction to the small aircraft.

She caught up and asked, “What, Jack? What is it?”

Jack glanced up with his eyes only. “It’s a government drone. I’m pretty sure it caught my image but someone who could recognize me would have to review the footage. It’s kind of a long shot, but it’s possible that they could make me.” He started forward, “Let’s get.”

Hanna nodded and they started off at a trot.

Chapter 40

Washington D.C.

Oval office

The first word reached the Oval Office at 5:00 pm EDT that something very wrong was happening in Homeless City.

Five minutes later, Atwood Colter arrived and entered the White House. He pushed open the President's door.

Fergusson barked, "What the fuck, Colter? What was in that vaccine? What's going on in Homeless City?"

"This can't be from the vaccine. It was just administered. It shouldn't be working yet. I've contacted Dale Feinberg and he told me that the vaccine that was sent to Homeless City was thoroughly tested. He said that what's going on there couldn't be from the vaccine."

"Famous last words... I've heard that we've lost all communications with Homeless City and that there is some kind of insurrection. Is that true?"

"Yes. I've just seen the drone footage. It appears that people from the Rehab Center and the Asylum have rebelled and are attempting to take control of the city. The streets are filled with dead. Some of the

Citizen Guards seem to have joined with the homeless."

"That doesn't make sense. I want to see the drone footage."

Colter nodded and moved to the President's computer and logged in under his own account. He typed in several commands then stood behind the President as the drone footage began.

The drone glided over a mountain top and descended towards the desert floor. In the distance, Homeless City appeared as a grey spot on the horizon. As the drone neared, it descended further towards the ground. The drone kept several hundred feet between itself and the ground. The ground was clearly visible and details there could be made out easily.

The drone approached the city and cleared a cyclone fence on the southwestern side. A road surrounding the city was just beyond the fence. There was no one on this side of the city. The road was deserted. As the drone cleared the road, it flew high between two buildings, and a woman in a gown and a man in a Citizen Guard uniform were the first people to be seen.

The drone passed and Colter squinted at the screen. "Wait," he said.

Fergusson turned and stared at him with a startled expression. "Wait for what?"

"May I?" Colter asked, reaching for the mouse on Fergusson's desk.

Fergusson shrugged.

Colter took the mouse and pulled the recorded video backward until the image was of a man and woman moving, the man stopping, and then glancing upward. Colter froze the frame of the man glancing up. While the picture was generally clear, the man's image was not perfectly revealed. He must have moved just enough to blur the frame. When Colter restarted the footage again, the man quickly looked downward.

"What is it, Atwood?"

"I'm not sure, but this guy looks like an old associate of mine. I've been trying to catch up with him. If it's the same guy? I'm going to need to have the image enhanced."

"Is this something that I should know about?"

"No. The guy's a rogue agent. We've been looking for him."

"Well, if he got the vaccine, he's probably going to be dead soon, anyway."

"Yeah, maybe, but this guy's slippery. If anyone would survive Homeless City, it would be him."

"Huh?" Fergusson said, then, "Not my problem. Let's look at the rest of this footage."

Colter nodded but was more interested in the missing Jack Morgan than in the chaos in Homeless City. Morgan had become an obsession.

The drone cleared a large one-story building and the main boulevard appeared in front of the Asylum and the Rehab Center.

The people visible were fighting. Those against the Citizen Guards were not using weapons. They bit and clawed and because they were in packs and groups, they seemed to be able to overwhelm the guards. Though most seem to have been shot several times, they were not detoured from their attacks.

Fergusson had a short attention span. He became bored and said, "I've seen enough. Handle this, Colter."

Colter nodded and knew that something was clearly wrong with everything that he had seen. He would need a better idea of what was happening in Homeless City. He had also heard about some strange happenings in Long Beach. Might be related, maybe not.

Chapter 41

Homeless City

Hanna and Jack continued to jog around the back of the city on the narrow, deserted road. When they came to streets that led to the main boulevard that led down the middle of the city, they stopped and observed to see if they might be attacked. In the far distance, on the boulevard, they could see people fighting in the streets. Whatever had begun at the Asylum and the Rehab Center had spread down the boulevard.

They reached the back of the first residential building that they encountered.

Jack said, "Let's see if we can find you some clothes."

Hanna nodded and Jack carefully pulled open a door in the back of the building. He peeked inside. People in grey jumpsuits with terrible wounds rushed towards the door. There were dozens in the long hallway attempting to get into the rooms. Jack slammed the door and locked it with a wave of his hand.

"Can't go in there," he said as bodies slammed into the door with unimaginable force. It was so violent that Hanna jumped back. Growls, hisses, and squawks could be heard as if an angry flock of some kind of deranged fowl slammed into a pride of lions. It was unearthly.

Jack said, “Let’s go.”

They continued around the first residential complex and then hustled past the next two. The cyclone fence here was tall and strong with razor wire atop. Lined up on the outside of the fence were several construction workers holding the fence with their fingers gripping it as if they would blow away if they let go.

Hanna froze as they neared the workers. Again, they all had white eyes and their clothes were in tatters as if they’d been mauled by mountain lions. Torn flesh showed through in places, nearly ripped to the bone.

When they saw Jack and Hanna, they instantly became agitated. Some began to growl and they followed Jack and Hanna with their nearly white eyes.

“Hanna,” Jack barked. “We need to keep moving.”

Hanna gave Jack a look that spoke of her confusion about what was happening.

Jack started out, staying close to the buildings.

One of the construction workers began shaking the fence and squawking loudly. Jack turned to see him begin to climb the fence. Other creatures also began doing the same. Jack stopped and watched as the first creature reached the razor wire.

The creature pushed at the wire and it bit deeply into the skin of his hand but he didn’t seem to notice. He began over as the others were reaching the top.

Jack stepped away from Hanna who was near the building and walked to the changed construction workers. He took aim and shot. Some fell back on the desert sand while others died entangled in the razor wire. Jack glanced around and several creatures dashed around the corner of the nearest street and ran directly at Hanna. She saw them and back-peddled, catching her foot on a rock. She fell flat on her back in a billow of now dried Asylum gown.

Jack sighted down the barrel of his gun and began firing. He emptied his clip as he smoothly ran towards Hanna, dropping the empty gun on the street then quickly pulling the next gun. As each creature neared Hanna, they dropped in a spray of brain matter.

Hanna had pushed up to her elbows, both now bleeding, and tried to scoot away. Jack kept firing emptying another gun, dropping it, and taking his last. Four more creatures were nearly upon Hanna. Jack used the next nine shots to finish the job but the last creature fell at Hanna's feet.

Jack breathed out with relief as he ejected the clip in the last gun and slammed in a loaded clip.

He jogged to Hanna.

She smiled wryly and said, "Well, that was a bit closer than I'd have liked."

Jack started to speak but just breathed out in relief instead.

The creatures who had been shot continued to move as if attempting to regain their lost abilities.

"I'm going to need to teach you how to shoot."

"Honestly, I can't wait."

"I have access to guns but we're going to need to get to LA."

Hanna nodded.

Jack retrieved his empty guns and reloaded each used clip. They then started back on their way around the outside of the city.

Chapter 42

Washington DC

The White House

Colter wasted no time. He needed to get back to his office at Langley and he needed to have the drone footage of Jack Morgan enhanced.

He called Edward Chang and had him begin the process of enhancing the film. Chang had access to the footage and he began his work as Colter continued the 16-minute drive down the George Washington Memorial Parkway.

Colter reached his building, jumped from the car, and hustled past security to his office. When he entered, he called Chang.

"Yes, Sir," Chang responded.

"Is the enhancing of the footage completed?"

"It is. It's in the folder marked "Enhanced Film" on your desktop display."

"Thanks."

Colter pulled up the film and fast-forwarded it to the man and woman on the screen. He enlarged the film to fill the screen then he stared and squinted at the image of the man. If it wasn't Jack Morgan, it was his twin.

Colter called Edward Chang back and asked, "Have we had any recent sightings of Jack Morgan?"

The last one was two days ago in the Netherlands."

"Huh. I want you to run a picture that I'm going to send you through facial recognition and see if this image matches the facial recognition file we have on Morgan."

"Will do, Sir."

Chapter 43

Langley Virginia

CGSS Headquarters

Ten minutes later, Atwood Colter received his answer. The image did not match the facial recognition file on Jack Morgan. Colter wasn't satisfied. He knew what his eyes had told him.

As he sat and pondered that bit of news. A message came in from Edward Chang.

Chang: "Need a meeting."

Colter: "Come now. At my office."

Edward Chang worked at what had now become known as the basement at Langley. It was where most of the data collection and state-sponsored hacking took place.

Chang exited the elevator and walked into Colter's outer office. The secretary buzzed him in.

Colter was sitting behind his desk. He knew that the situation in Homeless City was bad so he was prepared for nearly everything that Chang might say or so he thought.

"Hello, Mister Colter."

"Edward."

"I have something that I want to show you. I've been going over as much of the recorded film as we have at Homeless City near the moments where we lost contact. There's a lot of footage, 99 percent of it mundane. We record around two hours of film but do not save it. Around every two hours, we record over the previous film. It happens in a continuous loop. It was always thought that if we needed to see any earlier recordings, we could just go to the Homeless City servers and pull it up."

"Okay?"

"Obviously, we can't do that now."

"Yes?"

"This is some of what we still have. There is something very wrong with the people who are at Homeless City both Citizen Guards and residents. Or should I say, something has happened to them."

"Go on."

"I need to put this flash drive into your computer and show you the images that I have on it."

Colter slid his chair back and Chang slipped his flash drive into Colter's computer terminal. A file appeared and Chang opened it.

Chang said, "This was taken from two hours earlier than the footage I showed you before. Look closely at these people in the morgue."

"I'm looking. I don't see anything but autopsies."

"Just watch. Also, look at the time in the corner."

"Come on, Edward, I don't have all day."

Just then on the computer screen, the man on the autopsy table reached up and grabbed the throat of the coroner. The dead man's nearly white eyes opened wide and he pulled the coroner down and bit the coroner's neck taking a huge chunk of skin. Blood squirted from the wound and the coroner dropped. This happened so fast that a coroner working on a separate table in front of the dead coroner had heard his coworker falling and making a noise but he didn't respond. He only turned slightly then turned back to his work.

"I have no sound so if he said anything, it wasn't recorded."

The dead man being autopsied then rose on the stainless-steel table and slid to stand. He wasn't exactly steady at that moment so he paused.

"What the hell, Edward? The guy wasn't dead?"

"Look at the timer, boss."

Colter glanced at the timer in the corner of the screen. 22 seconds, 23 seconds, 24 seconds.

Then the coroner who had been bitten stood up and he and the dead man who had bitten him walked to the other coroner and attacked him, biting his neck. The dead woman that he was working on then sat up. Her chest and abdomen had been sliced open but nothing had yet been removed. She joined the attack on the now fallen coroner. The attack was savage. The three bit and clawed the fallen coroner but then the attack ceased and the fallen coroner rose and joined his attackers and the four walked from the morgue. The second coroner had half of his face ripped from the bone and his white apron and shirt were covered with his own blood. There were large rips in the material and hunks of skin missing from those places where the material of his clothes was torn.

Colter's mouth was open as he watched. He said, "I'm not processing this, Edward. I don't understand what I've just seen?"

"That makes two of us, Sir. So, empirically I would say that the people on the autopsy tables rose from the dead and bit and attacked the coroners who then joined them. The coroners were savagely attacked but not killed and though they should be writhing in pain from brutal wounds, they seemed as though nothing was wrong with them."

"Huh?"

"I'm going to venture a guess here, Mister Colter, that this is taking place all over Homeless City. This is why we saw on the drone video the insurrection and the fighting in the streets. I saw people shot, not fall, and continue their attack but it didn't register to me until now. By this time, there was so little footage that I could access from Homeless City, that I can't say for sure, that this is what's happening there but I would bet it is. Why else could a group of people in hospital gowns overrun well-armed Citizen Guards? Another thing, I believe that the communications with the city were deliberately shut down from inside the city and by an expert. Could the President have ordered the city to cut communications?"

"I don't believe so."

"Well, whoever shut down the communications was no rookie. That person was a real pro, more pro than me. We have been working to restart some communications with the city and have, so far, been unsuccessful."

"Jack," Colter whispered.

"Jack?"

"Morgan."

"Those files for facial recognition are standard. Is it possible that he got in and altered the files and corrupted them?"

"Anything is possible with Jack. He's probably the single most dangerous man on the planet with what he knows and his training."

"Training?"

"Jack has made quite a few of our countries enemies disappear, permanently. If you hear he's after you, you're having a bad day."

"Why did he go rogue? He sounds like a patriot."

"Let's just say that we had a difference of opinion about the scope of his job."

"I see," Chang said, then, "I'll go back to work on the communication problem in the city."

"Thanks. Leave me the flash drive. I have someone else to show it to."

Chang nodded and walked from the office.

Colter called President Fergusson.

Chapter 44

Washington DC

Oval Office

Twenty minutes later, Colter arrived at the White House. Fergusson was in a mood. It was two hours past the time he usually left the Oval Office and he didn't like to be there late.

When Colter entered, Fergusson said, "I hope this is good, Atwood."

"Only if you use the term loosely," Colter replied.

Fergusson glared.

Colter continued, "You need to see this." He held up a small flash drive.

Fergusson didn't respond as Colter walked to Fergusson's computer terminal and plugged the flash drive into the computer.

Colter then brought up the file and showed Fergusson the footage that he had just seen.

Fergusson said, "I don't understand what I just saw. It looked like the dead guys attacked the coroners and then the coroners joined them."

"That's what you saw."

"And this was in Homeless City?"

"That's correct."

"What's going on there?"

"We don't completely know. All communications have been cut off and the residents seem to be going mad and killing the guards and attacking each other. Then no one who has died, stays dead."

"You gave all of those people that vaccine," Fergusson said accusingly.

"I do not believe that this had anything to do with the vaccine. This is something unheard of."

"What now, Colter?"

"I've considered sending in a special forces team but after witnessing the footage, I don't think we could get them out alive. On the way here, I contacted Edwards Air Force Base to send another drone but this time not just for a flyover but to stay and give us a continuous feed. I'm afraid that what is happening there might be some kind of contagion."

"Like a virus?"

"I don't have any other explanation for what's happening. We can't call in any outside help, though, to figure it out in case..."

"In case what?"

"In case we need to eliminate the city."

Fergusson's eyes widened in shock. "Eliminate the city? It cost me a trillion dollars. What the fuck are you proposing, Colter?"

"I'm not proposing anything, yet. I just want our options open."

Fergusson sat in his chair and pulled the flash drive. He tossed it back to Colter.

Colter said, "If this is some kind of sickness, we can't let it get out into the country at large. And I don't think I need to tell you why."

"Let's wait for the footage," Fergusson said. He sat back in his chair with a distant stare.

Part 5

A Very Happy Accident...

Chapter 45

Death Valley, California

Homeless City

The north side of Homeless City was mostly residential. All the buildings that housed the population were connected by underground trains and walkways and were situated side by side. Because most people used the underground systems to get around, few people normally wandered the streets.

It had taken more than forty-five careful, painstaking minutes for Jack and Hanna to reach this point around the city. They had seen danger everywhere towards the main boulevard but encountered no more creatures on the fringes of the city.

As they passed the last few buildings, the mayhem that had been witnessed in the streets before was not as evident this far from the Asylum or the Rehab Center.

They reached Jack's building first with it being closer than Hanna's which was close to the Induction Center.

Hanna and Jack ran past Jack's building and then past several more residential complexes. The hope was that when they reached Hanna's building, the chaos might not have reached it so she could get her clothes.

It was twilight and as the city neared nightfall, it would potentially lead to different problems. More shadows for these creatures to spring from and as time passed, more creatures. Jack knew that if they didn't get out of the city soon, there would be no leaving at least not as a human.

They wound around the last residential building before reaching Hanna's apartment, then crossed the alley between. They quietly stepped to the back entrance of her building. Jack slowly opened the door and could see no creatures but the hallway was trashed. It appeared as though the people living here had vacated in a panic. Paper, garbage, some bath towels, washrags, and the occasional dropped piece of clothing lay upon the floor.

Jack turned back to Hanna. "This place looks deserted. Let's hustle to your room."

Hanna nodded and they jogged down the corridor. The hallways in each of the buildings were extremely long to fit as many residences as possible into each housing unit. All of the doors were close because the rooms were tiny. Each door had a number on it that denoted the building and room number.

They reached the final turn to the corridor that led to Hanna's room.

Hanna whispered, "It's this way. I live down here." She pointed.

Jack stopped and cautiously peered around the corner. He saw no one. He checked his gun to make sure it was fully loaded then he started towards Hanna's room. Several doors were kicked in and the frames splintered. He knew her apartment number so when they reached the room, he stopped and her door was damaged and ajar. He cautiously pushed it open. Someone had been inside. He glanced around but whoever it was had left.

He said, “Come in, Hanna, and change.”

Hanna nodded and went to her closet and pulled a jumpsuit. Two were hanging in her closet but her shoes were gone. She went to her dresser and all of her underclothes and socks were also gone.

“Huh?” she said questioningly. “Why did they take my underwear?”

Jack said, “Hurry, Hanna. We’ve got to get out of here.”

She nodded and pulled off her guard boots and the Asylum gown. Jack glanced at her. She had bruises, cuts, and scrapes on her elbows, back, and bottom.

“You’re pretty scraped up.”

Hanna turned and looked at her bare bottom and brushed at a bruise. She said, “I know. I can feel it.”

Without underclothes, she pulled on her grey jumpsuit and zipped the front, then put back on the guard boots while Jack checked his supply of ammo.

When Jack glanced back up, Hanna smiled wryly and said, “Well, this isn’t quite as airy as the hospital gown.”

He stared at her strangely.

“What?” she said.

He smiled, shook his head, stood, and peeked out the door. The hallway was still empty so he said, “Let’s go.”

He started out of the room and into the hallway sighting down the barrel of his gun. Hanna’s room was towards the front of the building so Jack started in that direction.

His mind was continuing to try to process what was happening. What had happened to all the people who lived in this building? Who had evacuated them? And where could they have gone?

They reached the front door that opened onto the boulevard. Its glass front gave a view from the gates at the entrance of "Homeless City, across the street to a security building and to the right for about a dozen residences.

Jack watched as ten of the creatures wandered down the middle of the boulevard in a pack. They moved slowly and with that same odd posture of something attempting to smell the air.

From down the street, Jack could hear the sound of motorcycles. The creatures stopped but didn't turn. Two Citizen Guards roared down the wide boulevard on their motorbikes. The creatures then turned towards the motorcyclists as they approached. The motorcyclists separated with one driving to the right around the creatures while the other went left. The one who went left moved easily around the creatures who were bunched in the middle of the street but the motorcycle that went right did not get far enough away from the creatures and two of them lunged at the racing bike. They struck it and the driver careened to the right then overcorrected back left and the bike went down. The creatures who jumped at the bike were violently thrown to the ground but the others with them who numbered eight quickly attacked the driver, biting, and clawing. The first two who jumped at the bike also rose and joined in the attack.

Jack watched as the driver seemed to die, then rose back up, changing within a minute of his attack. The creatures then left him alone and he and they started towards the Induction Center.

Hanna had come up beside Jack just in time to see the attack on the motorcycle rider.

She said, "What the hell is going on here, Jack? What kind of hell is this? I just don't understand?"

"I'm not sure either. I'm wondering if it has something to do with the vaccines. Nothing else makes sense." Then Jack nodded at the motorcycle lying in the middle of the boulevard. "That's our ticket out."

Hanna glanced down the street and more of the changed Homeless City residents were walking in their direction. Some were entering buildings but most were strolling with their noses pointed slightly upward, their heads slightly tilted to one side or the other, and that odd posture as if portions of their bodies were in some kind of spasm. All had gaping wounds beneath tattered gowns, grey jumpsuits, on naked bodies, or in Citizen Guard uniforms, and facial trauma that no plastic surgeon could repair.

From a building across the street, six Citizen Guards came out of the front door firing assault rifles at the creatures. All of the creatures who were in earshot turned to the gunfire.

Jack pushed Hanna to the ground fearing that she would be hit by a stray round. He put his body between her and the gunfire and he landed on her knocking the air from her lungs. High-powered rounds pinged off of the building and shattered windows.

Creatures fell when hit but most didn't stay down. They sprang up and ran with surprising speed at the Guards. The Guards could only be described as shocked. They seemed to freeze. It was apparent that they thought that their show of force would subdue the walking, changed humans but nothing could be further from the truth. As the creatures bolted for the Guards, the Guards resumed their assault. From left and right around corners, more creatures came at a dead-run for the Guards. The Guards all glanced around and could see the relentless charge. They had drifted from the door where they had emerged onto the street and a couple stopped shooting and ran back for the door but it was too late.

A mob of creatures reached them, overwhelming the six Guards, and began their fierce assault. The Guards flailed and fought but disappeared beneath the bodies of the creatures as they tackled and threw themselves at the Guards. The Guards had no chance. On the street, at least a dozen of the creatures lay unable to rise from head wounds but those not struck in the head seemed unharmed and in no pain.

Jack, laying in broken glass, crawled to the glass door. The top foot of the door was shattered leaving wandering cracks traveling down its length. Still on his stomach, he glanced down the wide boulevard. Hundreds, no thousands of creatures were emerging from the residences. None moving as fast as those who attacked the guards. Most were just sauntering as if out for a stroll on a Sunday afternoon.

"Wait here, Hanna. I'll be back for you."

Her eyes widened in fear for just a second, then she nodded.

"Here," he said, handing her a gun. "Point and fire. Aim for the head. Please try not to shoot yourself."

Jack checked one last time that the gun he was holding was fully loaded then he stepped out of the door and sprinted to the laying motorcycle. Several of the creatures took notice and started for him. He reached the motorcycle and raised it from the road. More creatures were starting for him. He tried to kick start the bike but it wouldn't start. He glanced down at the small control panel on the front of the bike and noticed a hand-pad.

Three of the creatures were closing in.

He turned and shot them. They dropped and Jack slapped his hand on the hand-pad. It lit green and then he kicked the starter and the bike sprung to life. By this time, no less than a hundred creatures had taken notice of Jack and the bike and they moved towards him, picking up speed, squawking, and growling.

Jack shot several more of the closing creatures then started away from the building where Hanna waited.

She couldn't believe her eyes as Jack disappeared around a building and it seemed as though he was heading out of town. The creatures followed him with surprising speed for their apparent lack of coordination.

Hanna waited for several minutes then began to panic. Jack appeared to have left.

"What am I going to do?" she thought aloud. "I'm toast."

Another few minutes passed and Hanna thought about trying to make it to the back of the Induction Center. Maybe people there had a plan to escape.

A sound like a motorcycle began low in the distance. Hanna turned back towards the door and looked through the bullet-ridden, double-paned glass, out onto the boulevard littered with bodies and the walking dead.

Jack turned the corner, traveling around 50 MPH, followed by creatures that had no hope of keeping up. He flew towards the place where the Citizen Guards had been killed and stopped and picked up an assault rifle. A hoard of creatures followed and began to catch up. He put some distance between himself and the creatures leading them away from Hanna's side of the street. He turned on a dime and raced back towards where Hanna waited. He waved at her to come outside as she stood at the glass door.

She stepped out and a male creature in a blood-soaked, grey jumpsuit, who had been close, came at her. She pointed the gun that Jack had given her but, in her panic, didn't seem to know how to pull the trigger.

Jack strafed the creature with the automatic assault rifle knocking it sideways and sending it careening into the building in a spray of mottled flesh. One of the rounds struck the creature in the head and it attempted to rise but could not.

Jack screeched to a stop near Hanna and said, "Get on! Hold on tight!"

She dropped the gun, climbed on the back of the motorcycle and they raced off.

More creatures attempted to cut them off by flooding out onto the boulevard but Jack fired the rifle cutting a hole through several of the creatures in the street. They wriggled and writhed and attempted to get back to their feet. One jumped at the motorcycle striking it near the front wheel but Jack held the bike firmly and ran over the creature. Looking through the rearview mirror, Jack could see the creature rise and stare at Jack and Hanna as they sped away. Jack raced through the rest of the creatures knocking some to the ground as he and Hanna sped past the Induction Center heading out of town. The assault rifle was empty of shells so Jack dropped it.

Hanna glanced over her shoulder and could see a few hundred creatures as they approached the Induction Center. A side door opened and residents who hadn't yet changed streamed out and onto a pavement parking lot. Creatures then came around the corners from the front and back. There would be no escape for the residents who had evacuated to the Induction Center.

Hanna laid her head on Jack's back and held on tight as he pushed the motorbike to 70 MPH.

They sped on the road and passed the construction site. Several of the changed creatures wandered around aimlessly and stared in Jack and Hanna's direction as they passed.

Five minutes later, they passed the old abandoned military base. No less than fifty creatures turned towards them and began to run in their direction but Jack stepped on the gas and streaked away.

He leaned back to Hanna and shouted, "Next stop, L.A."

Hanna nodded as the sun set in the California desert. She held on tightly around Jack's waist and rested her head on Jack's back.

Chapter 46

Langley, Virginia

Colter drove back to Langley in a kind of panic. He reached for his cell phone and contacted Edwards Air Force base as he drove.

"Give me General Hodges. This is Colter."

Colter waited.

"Yes, Mister Colter," General Hodges answered.

"Listen, Hodges, I need you to get a special forces unit into Homeless City and I mean yesterday. We need to grab a couple of those people wandering around the city and acting weird. Do you read me?"

"Yes, Mister Colter. I'm on it."

Colter hung up and thought, this is some kind of nightmare.

Chapter 47

Edwards Air Force Base, California

Two helicopters rose from the tarmac at Edwards Air Force Base. They turned northeast and sped towards Death Valley. The night was clear with nearly no cloud cover and a full moon rose above, lighting the ground below. The moon had just cleared the mountains to the east and its orb was large and bright against the night sky.

The choppers descended to the valley floor. They quickly reached Homeless City. There were no lights in the city and from a distance, it looked every bit dead.

The choppers approached from the southwest with floodlights lighting the ground and did not land behind the razor wire fence. They continued to where the large wide boulevard split the city in half. Here, the fence was open to the desert as the boulevard stretched from the city and became a narrow two-lane, rural road heading out.

The pilots could see people wandering aimlessly in their floodlights. As the choppers approached, the people on the ground took notice and seemed to become agitated. Their white eyes lit with animal eyeshine and they followed the sound of the copters with their attention and every time the helicopters came close to the ground, the people near bunched in anticipation of their landing.

The pilots could see that the people were in all states of dress from nude to fully dressed Citizen Guards but every person's clothes were ripped and torn. They all had ghastly injuries.

The helicopters pulled back and a crowd followed them. They circled the main boulevard and as they did so, the people on the ground followed the choppers. They never took their white eyes from the circling flying machines, eerily looking upward, watching as they flew, seeming to hope they would land.

The pilot shook his head at Lieutenant Francis Graton, the officer leading the mission, sitting next to him. Graton called to the accompanying chopper and said, "Are you seeing what I'm seeing?"

"Affirmative, Francis. What the hell?"

"Don't know. We're going to need to land farther away. Maybe we can find a couple of strays. Let's make a wider circle and see if someone has wandered from the city."

"Roger."

The two choppers made a circle once around the interior of the city. Every place they went, the reaction of the people on the ground was the same. They bunched and looked up in anticipation of the choppers' landing. Lieutenant Graton had specific orders, however, to avoid any crowd, though he wasn't sure why. His special forces were armed to the max.

As they widened their circle, they could see small packs of individuals wandering in all directions. These people had obviously come from the city. They were a mixture of Citizen Guards, grey jump-suited residents, people in hospital gowns, and the occasional nude.

The copters continued to search for a couple of people moving together and away from any of the other residents. They came across two people, one male in a grey jumpsuit and a female in a hospital gown. They were both barefooted and walking easily across the rocky desert floor. Both of their clothing was ripped in places. The male's jumpsuit was blood-soaked. The female's hospital gown was torn in places but only had blood around her collar as if she had tried to drink the red liquid and spilled it on herself. They walked away from the city with a kind of aimlessness that gave the appearance of mindlessness. They were walking together but did not have the appearance of being together.

The special forces copters came in low and the two people on the ground stopped and gazed upward. Their eyes fixed on the choppers.

"There's our targets," Graton announced.

The special forces units in both copters readied to snatch the two wanderers.

"Let's get these two alive," Graton commanded. "You know the drill."

The choppers hovered together some fifty yards away from the wandering residents. The soldiers inside the helicopters readied to deploy rapidly and thought that they might have to run down these two who might try to avoid capture but as the choppers neared the ground, the two people ran towards them.

Graton speculated that they were maybe wanting to be picked up. Before the choppers landed, the side doors on both simultaneously opened and the special forces jumped to the ground. No one was sure what to expect. They had orders to subdue one or two of the wandering citizens of the city and bring them back for study. Graton thought that this would be an easy abduction and they could head back home.

Once on the ground, the special forces Sargent yelled, "Halt," to the two now sprinting Homeless City residents.

The two units converged on the sprinting couple.

"Get ready," the Sargent commanded to his troops then shouted, "Halt!" at the sprinting residents of Homeless City.

They did not even slow.

Two special forces men holding tasers pointed them at the charging people. When the two people got to within twenty-five feet, they both let loose the tasers. They struck both rushing people flat on their chests.

Nothing happened.

The eyes of both the residents were white and wild. Their mouths opened and their teeth flashed in the light of flashlights trained upon them.

"Should we shoot?" one of the soldiers asked. There were just moments left before the charging people would reach the soldiers.

"No," the Sargent commanded. "Just tackle them and we'll bind them and take them back."

The two residents reached the soldiers and the soldiers gang tackled the two. The two were inhumanly strong and they bit and fought.

"Shit," one of the soldiers shouted. "One of the bastards bit me."

He rubbed at a slight abrasion on his neck.

Another soldier agreed, rubbing a slight abrasion on his wrist.

In less than a minute, the two residents were subdued and their arms and legs bound with plastic restraints, the Sargent barked, "Get them in the choppers! Move it, people!"

The two residents were thrust unceremoniously onto the floor of one of the copters. They twisted and writhed and snapped their jaws as if they were wild escapees from an unknown world. Their white eyes bulged and red animal eyeshine reflected in their stare when their eyes came in contact with the ambient light of the chopper. The special forces soldiers then jumped into both choppers and they were off.

"Let's get out of here," Lieutenant Graton barked.

Both choppers rose as more residents of Homeless City had taken their notice and moved in their direction. Some were sprinting but others strolled as if walking in the park on a Sunday afternoon.

The copter that held the captives had the Lieutenant, the Sargent, and four other Special Forces soldiers. The other chopper held eight soldiers which included the two who had been bitten. The helicopters turned together and started back towards Edwards.

Without warning, the two soldiers who had been bitten suddenly leaped at the soldiers sitting closest to them. The irises in their eyes had turned light and they bit and clawed. The other soldiers had no idea what was happening. They thought that it was some kind of dispute between the soldiers. But within a few seconds, the soldiers who had been bitten turned on other of the soldiers then they continued to attack until all of the soldiers in the chopper had been changed. Next, they attacked the pilots.

One pilot shouted, "What the fuck?!" Then, "Hey!?" Then, "Help, we're being attacked! We're going down!"

The chopper began to spin as if suddenly out of control. It lurched at the other chopper carrying the Lieutenant and the residents of Homeless City.

The other chopper took evasive action and barely avoided a mid-air collision. Collision alarms blared.

The Lieutenant watched as the out-of-control chopper careened under his and slammed into the desert floor below in a ball of fire. Several of the soldiers walked from the crashed chopper, fully in flames, and collapsed on the sand, yards from the wreckage.

"Holy shit," the Lieutenant whispered in shock.

His captives continued to growl, arch, and twist, and their teeth gnashed and clicked as they snapped.

The Lieutenant turned to the Sargent and said, "What the hell's going on here?"

The Sargent shook his head and said, "I have no idea, Sir."

Chapter 48

Jack and Hanna continued to ride on the nearly deserted Highway 190 away from Homeless City. They passed Stovepipe Wells and Jack glanced down at his gas gauge. Nearly full. That was good news since he had no money. At some point, he would probably need to steal a car.

Hanna tapped Jack's shoulder. "Jack, I have to pee."

He nodded and pulled off the road. It was full dark by this time and there wasn't a headlight in sight but the moon was full and threw silvery light, illuminating the surrounding desert.

Hanna said, "Um. Here?"

"Yeah. Hurry. We need to get to the next semi-large town so I can borrow a car. This may not get us where we need to go."

"Borrow a car? Who's going to lend you their car?"

"Anyone, since they won't know until after the fact."

"Steal a car?! You mean steal!?"

"Yeah. Well, we don't have any money or identification and we're around 4 hours from L.A."

"Yeah, but, steal a car!? Geez, Jack."

"Don't worry. We won't hurt the car and I'll leave it where it will be found and not stripped. I'll even call the people it belongs to and thank them."

"You will?"

"No. Now go pee so we can get back on the road."

"So, what happens when we get to L.A.?"

"I have resources there. We'll be fine. Now go pee."

Hanna nodded, looked around, unzipped her jumpsuit, slipped it off her shoulders, and pulled it down, then did her business. She climbed back on the bike behind Jack, wrapped her arms around him, then they were back on the road.

As they were picking up speed, Hanna said, "I miss underwear."

Jack laughed.

Chapter 49

Death Valley, California

The remaining special forces' helicopter raced back to Edwards Air Force Base. When it landed, a team with one doctor, three nurses, and two gurneys waited.

The blades slowed and under the full moon, the special forces team pulled the two hostages who were straight out of a nightmare from the wide side chopper doors and laid them onto the gurneys being careful to not get bitten and strapped them down. The two Homeless City residents with white eyes bulging, continued to snap, growl, and squawk.

Under the slowing blades, Lieutenant Graton shouted to the medical team, "Don't get near them, they bite!"

Captain Samuel Clark hustled to the chopper as the blades began to slow.

Graton saluted as his commander approached. He loudly said, "I don't know what we have here, Captain, but that city is filled with these things. I didn't see anyone who was normal. By the way, two of my team were bitten by them. They were on the chopper that went down."

Captain Clark replied, "We're examining the feeds from the body cams right now to try to determine what happened on the second chopper. What were the names of the two who were bitten?"

"Blake and Jimenez."

"Alright. You're dismissed. We'll get together in one hour."

Graton checked his watch, saluted, and then joined his remaining men.

"Another thing you need to consider," Graton said, turning back.

"What's that?"

"Those things are wandering from the city."

Captain Clark seemed to pale. He nodded and turned away.

Graton and what was left of his team walked downcast from the tarmac.

The medical team that now had the two hostages were in gloves, face masks, and face shields. They wheeled the two residents of Homeless City into the building and to a medical station.

Captain Clark caught up with Captain Laura McBride who was the attending physician. She watched with wide eyes as her new patients fought and struggled against their restraints. The medical team rolled the gurneys close to each other then made sure that the strapped restraints that they had placed over the plastic restraints were on tightly. The man was in a grey jumpsuit and every muscle on his body was taught as he tirelessly fought against his restraints. The woman was in a hospital gown and she did the same.

Captain Clark said, "Let me know when you know something."

They both stared at the two people from Homeless City as they growled and fought against their restraints. Clark and McBride glanced at each other having no idea what they were witnessing.

McBride nodded and Clark jogged off to his debriefing with his special forces team.

The medical team then rolled the two gurneys from the tarmac and to a small medical station near the airfield.

Doctor McBride said, "We need to get blood. Get a sample from both. Stay away from their mouths."

The team jumped to it.

McBride looked closely at each of her patients as they struggled. The man had gaping wounds where he had been repeatedly bitten. Large rips and holes in his clothes revealed flesh torn to the bone. He must have had massive blood loss at some point because his clothes were covered in the substance.

The woman had no bite marks but had a deep slash on her abdomen that should have bled profusely but no blood seemed to leak from the wound.

The nurse with the woman said, "Doctor, there's no blood in her veins."

Doctor McBride said, "Huh?" She was lost in thought as she stared at her patients, not fully listening. "Say again."

"No blood at all. Nothing."

The second nurse said, "No blood in this one either."

For a second, all three stood and stared at each other not speaking.

McBride turned and walked to a roll-around tray. She lifted a scalpel and walked back to the man on the gurney. She then pushed the scalpel into the forearm of the male patient and cut a small incision. The man did not flinch and he also did not bleed.

“What the hell?” one of the nurses quietly exclaimed.

“What the hell indeed,” McBride echoed.

She cut a small piece of tissue from the man and placed it in a specimen container then did the same to the woman. Then she said, “Cut off their clothes, and let’s give them a good going over.”

One nurse lifted scissors from the tray and began cutting the jumpsuit from the man and the other nurse did the same to the woman.

The first nurse looked at the now nude woman and said, “Are you going to try to stitch up this wound?”

The doctor stared at a deep cut on the woman’s abdomen.

McBride looked bewildered. She said, “Right now, I don’t know.” She glanced at the now nude man and could see that the skin on his upper thigh was ripped and hanging down to his knee. The femur was exposed. She then said, “I don’t know what to do.”

McBride then called for another nurse to run the specimens to the lab. She continued her examination of the two people from Homeless City. No internal organs were functioning. No heartbeat or pulse. The temperature of the patients was 75 degrees Fahrenheit just slightly above the temperature in the medical facility. These people were, in effect, dead, though they seemed to gasp in air as they growled and squawked. Without blood, though, there couldn’t be any transfer of oxygen to the cells.

McBride ordered an EEG to check their brain waves. The readings were all off the charts. Something was occurring in the patient’s brains but it wasn’t normal. There was activity but the activity was filled with spikes as if the patients were suffering from constant seizures. Most of the brain was not fully functioning, though the hindbrain had the most activity.

General Hodges had just spoken with Captain Clark. He burst into the examination room where the two hostages from Homeless City were being examined.

He barked, "What do we have here, McBride?"

"Damned if I know," she said.

The General stopped in his tracks as he caught his first glimpse of the two changed people as they struggled and growled.

McBride said, "You might want to suit up before you come in here, General. We think this might be contagious."

General Hodges paled at those words. He turned on his heels and walked out.

McBride followed him and said, "We're running tests right now. I have never seen anything like this or heard of anything like this except for maybe demonic possession."

Hodges didn't smile at the jest.

"Listen, General, I don't know what to do with these two."

The general peeked through a glass window in the door. He saw one of the creatures try to bite one of the nurses as she walked by.

McBride continued, "I have no idea how these people are alive or functioning. Their body temperature is 75 degrees. They have no flowing blood in their veins, none of their internal organs are functioning except for their brains. Their brains are firing as if they are having continual severe seizures and only their hindbrains seem to be fully functioning.

I truly do not know what I'm dealing with. If you were to ask me, I'd say that these people are not from this planet. When cut, they do not bleed. It's as if something is controlling their bodies but I don't see how."

"I need to call the President," the General said quietly. Then he said, "Do not discuss this with anyone. Do you read me?"

"Loud and clear, General. What now?"

"I'll send someone to take these people somewhere. I'll get back to you. Keep them out of sight."

"Yes, Sir."

The General turned on his heels and stomped from the room.

A half-hour later, the results of the samples that went to the lab came back and were inconclusive, no known virus, no known bacteria, and no known parasite. There was no pathogen of any kind detected. She then took additional samples from the patients and had them sent to UCLA Medical Center for a more extensive analysis. Doctor McBride's next thought was to notify the Center for Disease Control but she had been ordered to keep it quiet. She was frightened and could feel the fear deep in the pit of her stomach. This didn't make sense and that cold fear settled in every part of her body.

Chapter 50

Jack and Hanna raced down Highway 190 until it turned into Panamint Valley Road then continued on until that road became Trona Wildrose Road. The moon was still full, the night mild, and the miles between them and Homeless City grew. The landscape here was bleak and they saw few cars pass.

The fuel gauge showed a little less than two-thirds of a tank so Jack had some miles to play with but he was concerned that he wouldn't make it to L.A. on the one tank. It would be close but it wasn't a sure thing.

They passed several small towns and Jack decided to press his luck and drive all the way to L.A. If they ran out of gas, he would then have to steal a car. The miles rolled past.

Chapter 51

Edwards Air Force Base, California

General Hodges, Captain Clark, and Lieutenant Graton stood together in the General's office.

The General began the meeting, "Lieutenant, first let me say how sorry I am for the loss of part of your team. That's always a difficult thing to deal with."

"Thank you, General. They were good men."

"Give me a quick overview of what happened on your mission."

"Yes, Sir. We came in and flew over a portion of the city looking for a couple of individuals to bring back here. The city is packed with these changed people. Every time we dropped in altitude, a group of people gathered below us. It was eerie. They would all stand together in a bunch and stare up with those white eyes. Sometimes their eyes would flash like an animal at night. I decided to skirt the city and look for a couple of people that were away from the others. That's when we came upon the two that we brought back."

"So, is it your opinion that the entire city is full of these, whatever they are?"

"It looked like it to me, thousands of them and it also appeared as though they were leaving the city.

Not in droves but in trickles, a couple here and a couple there, but they are beginning to leave."

"Thanks, Lieutenant, you can go. I need to make a phone call. You can go too, Captain."

Graton and Clark saluted and walked from the room.

Hodges lifted the phone. He spoke to his secretary, "Get me Atwood Colter."

A minute later, Colter was on the line. "Atwood. We have a real problem in Homeless City, one that I'm afraid might spread. We've captured two of the residents from there and they have changed into something that we do not understand."

Colter was silent.

Hodges continued, "They have no blood in their veins though they seem to breathe to take in air. Their organs no longer are functioning and most of the brains in each are also not functioning except for elevated activity in the hind regions, and they are having brain wave spikes as if they are in a constant state of seizure. Honestly, it's like something has taken over their bodies. Their eyes are white as if they're blind but they seem to see, though we can't be sure. They are enormously strong as if on a full adrenaline charge."

The General stopped his monologue but Colter still didn't respond.

"Mister Colter?"

"Yes, I'm here... General, there are nearly one million people in that city. I've seen them attack and overwhelm seasoned well-armed Citizen Guards, though shot multiple times."

"What's the plan, Mister Colter?"

"I need to talk to the President."

Colter hung up and stared out and around his office without seeing.

He called President Fergusson.

As usual, Fergusson did not want to be bothered. He was watching a golf tournament.

Fergusson said impatiently, "Yes yes. What is it?"

"This is Colter, Donald. We have a real problem in Homeless City." He outlined everything that General Hodges had told him then he said, "There are nearly one million of these change people in that city. If they get out, I'm not sure we could stop this contagion if that's what it is."

"Should we send in the Army?"

"That would give too many people knowledge of what's going on there."

"What are you proposing, Atwood?"

"An accident. A happy accident. Nearly no one has any idea that Homeless City even exists."

Fergusson paused for a heartbeat then said, "Can you arrange that? I don't want to be linked to it in any way."

"Consider it done."

"We'll talk afterward."

Fergusson hung up.

Colter continued to stare, deep in thought. He would need a plausible alibi. He called General Hodges back.

Chapter 52

Los Angeles, California

Jack and Hanna entered L.A. the next morning just before sunrise. The motorcycle was on fumes but had delivered them all the way. Jack pulled into a park near a storage facility in East L.A. This was a well-known, high-crime neighborhood. He pulled into a parking place by a small park with basketball courts and children's swings. Streetlights lit portions of the sidewalks but left dark places between. Though early in the morning, several people wandered the park, all appearing shady. Two guys in their late teens and looking for trouble approached Jack and Hanna. They were heavily tattooed and approached with attitude.

"Hey, man, nice bike."

"You want it, it's yours," Jack said, smiling.

One of the teenagers half-smiled at his friend as if to say, I'll teach this old fuck a lesson. Then he snapped, "You fucking with me, man! What else you got? How about that bitch. I could use her." The teen grabbed his crotch while his friend reached behind his back.

Before the teens could blink, Jack pulled two pistols from his jacket pockets and stuck them in the teens' faces. "I got these," he sneered. His face was tight and his eyes murderous.

“Fuck, man!” the first teen said, taking a step back. His friend looked as though he would faint. It wasn’t just that Jack had pulled the guns, it was the attitude he projected that he wouldn’t hesitate to use them, an attitude not lost on the youths.

Jack softly said through clenched jaws, “Don’t piss me off.”

“No way, man. Thanks for the bike if you still giving it to me.” The teens knew that the bike had been stolen since it was a Citizen Guard bike.

Jack smiled menacingly, lowered his guns to his side, and he and Hanna walked off. Jack walked backward for several steps watching the wayward youths.

The teens turned and walked back to the bike. One made a phone call.

Hanna said, “Geez! That was scary. I thought you might give me away.”

“Not to them. I was thinking about it back when I needed gas. There’s lots of small bars where you might have got me enough cash to fill the tank.”

“Hahaha, bastard. You’re picking up my dark sense of humor.”

Jack smirked.

“I thought you might kill those kids.”

“They had a 50/50 chance. They were smarter than they acted. I had a feeling that I could convince them of the errors of their ways, besides, I didn’t want all the noise of blowing them away. I didn’t have silencers. I wouldn’t have killed them had they pushed it, but they wouldn’t be walking any time soon. I would have shot the one in the shoulder who reached behind his back and kneecapped the other, then I would have shot the guy holding his shoulder in his leg so they wouldn't follow."

"Oh," Hanna said quietly.

They continued two blocks to a storage facility. Jack punched a code into a keypad by an iron gate and the gate rolled open. He and Hanna stepped inside and the gate closed behind them. They walked to one of three, one-story, orange-painted buildings in a line with driveways between them. Most of the units had roll-up doors that could be accessed from outside the building.

The building that Jack approached, did not. Jack punched the same code into another keypad and the door to the building unlocked with a click. He opened the door and walked down a long, dim hallway to storage unit 232. He punched in the same code again and the roll-up door on the unit began to ascend.

"I need to get a couple of things in here. Then I'll have access to more of the resources that I have scattered around."

Hanna nodded and peered inside as the door reached the top of the unit.

The unit contained several boxed items, a cot with a rolled-up sleeping bag sitting atop, and several things covered in tarps.

Jack opened a small box and took out several thousand dollars in cash. He took credit cards and identification cards with different aliases and a small laptop computer. He went to an upright locker against the back wall and took out a shotgun. Hanna peeked inside and could see enough ammo to supply a small army.

Hanna asked, "You sleep here sometimes?"

"I have, but it's not my first choice." He smiled then unloaded the two handgun clips that he had been using from Homeless City. He set the guns in his locker.

"Not bringing these guns?" Hanna pointed.

"No. They are Citizen Guard issued handguns. I don't want to be caught with them. I have my own."

Jack then tucked a box of shotgun shells into his pocket. He took off the belts that he had strapped over his shoulders and placed all of the bullets from the belts into a backpack and gave it to Hanna.

"Put this on," he instructed.

She did so. The backpack was heavy.

He grabbed another handgun of his own and put it in a shoulder holster, then he took a small-caliber handgun from his locker and handed it to Hanna.

She held it and gazed over its surface.

"This will do for you," he said. He took it back and slipped it into the backpack. "I'll give this to you when I'm fairly sure you won't accidentally shoot me."

She smiled and nodded.

Happy with his armament situation, Jack then pulled a tarp off of another motorcycle. It was smaller than the one that they used to escape from Homeless City. He slipped the shotgun into a place on the side of the bike and pushed the bike into the hallway.

He said, "Let's go get some sleep."

"Okay? Where?"

"You'll see."

Jack smiled, handed Hanna a helmet, and took one for himself. Then after closing and locking his unit, he pushed the bike out of the building and through the gate. The streets were deserted. Jack got on the bike and Hanna climbed on behind him. He started the bike and they left for somewhere unknown.

Chapter 53

Langley, Virginia

Two hours later, Atwood Colter waited in his 8600 square foot, luxury mansion for word from General Hodges. He was sitting on a leather couch in his large office, sipping brandy, and watching the state-sponsored news with the government-fed content. He smiled at the crap.

A beep repeated from the phone with a secure line. He rose and picked up the receiver.

The voice of General Hodges said, “The Eagle is in the air.”

Colter replied, “Thank you.” He replaced the receiver, did not contact the President, and went to bed...

Chapter 54

Los Angeles, California

Jack pulled into a small motel off of highway 405 near LAX. Both he and Hanna were exhausted. It was a shabby establishment and could use a coat of paint. Mounds of litter had blown in places and stuck to the cyclone fence that separated its parking lot from the surrounding buildings.

Jack left Hanna with the bike while he checked in. When he came back, he said, “Room 42.”

She glanced around, “Nice place. You know how to impress.”

The motel backed up to a housing project in what was obviously a high-crime area.

“Nothing but the best for my ladies.”

“Ladies? Plural?”

“I have a business relationship with the guy who works the desk here. He doesn’t ask any questions and I pay generously with cash.”

“And your ladies?”

Jack shrugged and smiled.

They drove to room 42 which was towards the end of the building, climbed off of the bike, and walked into the room. It was clean but decorated in dark colors to not show the stains. It had the odd smell of camphor. Jack threw his shotgun onto the bed.

Hanna sat down next to it and looked around while Jack plugged in his laptop. Hanna reached for the TV remote and channel-surfed for a minute. She landed on a softcore porn movie with lots of motion but few body parts. She watched for a minute then turned on a news channel with a host praising President Fergusson for his many great accomplishments, decisions, and ideas.

Jack pulled up his sign-on screen and signed-in to his laptop. He then poked around looking for information about Homeless City. He didn't find anything new but he had an idea that there was information out there that he should know but he was tired and could hardly keep his eyes open.

Hanna said, "I need a shower."

"Me too," Jack agreed. "You go ahead."

"Really, Jack. I was thinking that I would like to shower with the guy who just saved my life. I would really like to thank him."

Jack smiled, stood, and slipped off his shirt.

Twenty minutes later, Jack and Hanna slipped into the motel bed. They laid down, both nude and now clean from their traumatic day. Hanna put her arm around Jack and cuddled to him. They both fell quickly to sleep without the promised special thank you.

The news droned on in the background...

Chapter 55

Area 51, Nevada

The two changed people abducted from Homeless City were flown to Area 51, a remote attachment of Edwards Air Force Base in Nevada. They rushed them to an underground facility and quickly to an operating room. There, they were each strapped down onto an operating table and killed. The researchers were shocked to find the difficulty in attempting to kill the two subjects. Lethal injections did not work. An attempt to cut their jugular veins did not work and other more barbaric attempts also did not work. Finally, they had to remove the brains of each.

Once the subjects had been finally terminated, extensive autopsies were then performed with samples of lung, heart, brain, and the rest of the internal organs sent back to UCLA Medical Center for further tests. The results to be sent to Atwood Colter.

Chapter 56

Los Angeles, California

Jack woke first. He was disoriented. The drapes were pulled so that it was nearly black in the room but for a sliver of light from outside that leaked through a slight parting in the middle. He rolled to his side and saw Hanna sleeping deeply with the covers pulled up to her chin.

He rubbed his face. The TV was still on and tuned to the news station that Hanna had put on before they fell asleep.

Hanna seemed to sense that Jack had awoken and she cracked an eyelid. "Hey," she said sleepily.

"Good morning," Jack responded.

She reached over and hugged Jack to her. She let her hand roam his back then rested it on his backside. She kissed him.

"I got to pee," she said.

Jack smiled and Hanna got up. He enjoyed the view of her fully nude as she walked away.

He turned to the TV and clicked up the volume a bit. The picture was of what appeared to be a mushroom cloud. Something had seriously exploded.

The news announcer said, "... Accident in the desert near Death Valley."

"What!?" Jack said, standing, still nude himself.

Hanna walked from the bathroom and said, "What did you say?"

"Shhh."

"What is it?"

Jack's eyes were glued to the TV. He said, "I got to check something."

He walked directly to his computer while Hanna crawled back into bed and watched the newscast. The reporter was talking about some kind of plane crash in the desert. The plane was carrying high explosives and it appeared as though had detonated.

"This is some kind of accident," Hanna said matter-of-factly as she watched the broadcast.

"In the middle of Death Valley? Right where we were?!"

"Oh. Umm... Geez."

"That looked atomic but planes don't carry live weapons in case they do crash."

"The reporter said that it was high explosives."

"Huh?"

He pulled up Atwood Colter's account but could find nothing new. He scoured his information sites but there was nothing that he could glean that would infer that this wasn't an accident.

He said, "I can't find anything but I'd bet my testicles that this was no accident."

"Don't bet those."

"I think they blew Homeless City. It was out of control and there was something very scary going on there, something that I don't think they anticipated."

"So, they nuked it?"

"I think so. We need to get on the road."

"On the road? To where?"

"San Francisco after a pit stop."

Hanna glanced at the clock. She said, "It's 4:30. We slept most of the day. Kind of late for a motorcycle ride to San Francisco. Besides, my butt is sore from the ride from Homeless City. I don't think I could handle 7 hours on the back of a bike again."

"I have a car in Santa Clarita with a friend. We will drive there, sleep, then in the morning, head to the city."

"Who's the guy?"

"Not a guy."

"Ohhhh. Umm... Well..."

"An old friend and associate."

"One of your ladies?"

Jack shrugged.

"How much friend and how much associate?"

"About the same of each."

"Could you be more cryptic?"

"What do you want to know, Hanna?"

"What do you think? Is she your girlfriend?"

"No."

"Was she your girlfriend?"

"Not exactly."

"Friends with benefits?"

Jack smiled.

"Ah-ha."

"Way to go, Sherlock."

"So, you had a relationship of a sexual manner with this lady."

"Yeah, but she would probably be more interested in you than me."

"So, she's a lesbian?"

"She's a free spirit. She had been living with another woman the last time I saw her."

"Jack, you stinker! You did unspeakable things with her and her friend?"

"Unspeakable means that you don't speak of them. So, no comment."

"Bastard."

Jack laughed.

"Is she government?"

"No, freelance."

"Freelance what?"

"She's a hacker, a gifted one. She'll maybe have some information or will know how to get some, but she doesn't have the government access that I do. She hangs around in darker places."

"But she likes sex," Hanna said accusingly.

"You seem to be hung up on that aspect of her."

"Yeah, well, that's because I've taken a liking to you and I shouldn't be jealous but..."

"She's different from most people. How can I explain her? She's very, umm, what's the word I'm looking for, *curious*. She likes to observe anything she shouldn't see. Sometimes she'll hack into corporate meetings or government meetings. If someone catches her interest for any reason, she'll begin digging and won't quit until she has witnessed something so personal that the person would be mortified if they knew. People leave their laptops on all the time. She has popped into many a bedroom and seen a lot of very private moments."

"Huh? What does she do with the information she collects?"

"She isn't like other hackers. She is incredibly wealthy though she lives in a modest house in a modest neighborhood with a detached garage in the back. That's where I keep my car and some other things. The things she collects in her hacking just live in her mind. She has a photographic memory. She doesn't record anything and she doesn't blackmail. She's just a voyeur."

"Strange."

"Yep. She's an odd one." Jack smiled, then said, "Let's get dressed."

"Not yet. I have a frightful urge and since you're already naked..."

She rose from the bed, walked to Jack, sat on his lap, then kissed his lips...

Chapter 57

Langley, Virginia

Atwood Colter contacted the President. Colter's first words were, "It's finished."

Fergusson asked, "Any known survivors?"

"We are checking now, but I don't believe so."

"And what of the city?"

"Down to the foundations."

"Problem solved?"

"I think so."

"Don't just think so, Atwood. Know so."

Colter hung up but was not so sure that it was over. How it happened, whatever it was, was still a mystery. And that was the problem.

Chapter 58

Santa Clarita, California

Santa Clarita lies over 1000 feet above the LA basin. It sits on Interstate 5 just past the end of the Grapevine, the 40-mile-long mountain pass that connects Southern California to the San Juaquin Valley near Bakersfield.

Jack exited Interstate 5 at McBean Parkway and drove into a residential area on the outskirts of Santa Clarita. The tree-lined street was quiet with cars parked in driveways and neat yards. He pulled into his friend's driveway and parked next to a new, dark blue BMW. As he and Hanna climbed off of the bike, Lacey Pembroke stepped out of the front door.

She was lean, dressed in a low-cut yellow tank-top, braless, barefoot, and in short shorts with a thin stripe down the sides. Her skin was tanned as if she spent a lot of time on the beach. She was attractive, outdoorsy, and appeared to be in her late thirties or early forties. Her brown hair was cut short and spiked with a hint of red at the tips. She had an array of tattoos on her legs, arms, and back with one lone tattoo on her neck under her ear and one on her right breast, partially hidden by her lowcut shirt.

Her eyes lit with delight. "Jaaack!" She dragged out his name.

"Hi, Lacey."

"Been a while."

"I've had a few complications."

Lacey walked to Jack and hugged him then kissed his lips... The kiss was a bit too long for just friends.

He smiled. "It's good to see you."

"You too," she responded in a sultry manner, then said, "And who is this lovely lady?"

"Lacey, I'd like you to meet Hanna."

Lacey approached Hanna and hugged her tightly and then quickly kissed her cheek.

Jack said, "I need to pick up a few things."

"Awe, I thought you came to see me."

"I'm always happy to see you, you know."

"I know."

Another young woman slipped out of the front door and stood on the porch. She couldn't be more than twenty with pale skin, blond mussed hair, and pouty lips. She was sultry and looked as though she just came from bed and she probably did. Her clothes clung to her body. She was wearing shorts and a tee-shirt made of thin material that seemed to reveal everything beneath.

"This is Tiffany."

"Hi," Tiffany said, then turned and walked back inside.

"Where's Annette?" Jack softly asked.

"She began to bore me, so, she had to go. Come in, Jack and Hanna. Let's have a glass of wine."

Jack smiled again and said, "Sounds good."

Lacey walked into her house followed by Jack and Hanna. She lit a cigarette, took a drag, walked into the kitchen, and began opening a bottle of red wine.

Tiffany was barefoot and walked to a chair across the room. She had the look of someone open to nearly anything. She sat Indian-style on the chair and leaned over and lit a joint. The haze of smoke began to linger in the unmoving air.

Jack and Hanna sat on a couch that faced a kitchen counter. Tiffany stood and passed her joint to Hanna. Hanna took a hit and passed it to Jack who also took a hit and passed it back to Tiffany.

Tiffany stood then and walked to Lacey who was placing wine glasses on the counter and pouring the wine. Tiffany rested her hand on Lacey's shoulder, caressing it slightly. She glanced at Hanna and Jack and the look in her eyes said, "Yes, Lacey and I are fucking." She handed Lacey the joint. Lacey took a drag then handed it back.

Jack asked, "Can we crash here tonight?"

Lacey replied, "I was counting on it."

Jack smiled again and glanced at Hanna who smirked back.

"So, Jack, what's going on?" Lacey asked, bringing the wine to Hanna, Jack, and Tiffany.

Tiffany had passed the joint around one more time then finished it. Her eyes were drooping.

"I've been living in the twilight zone for a few weeks."

"Twilight zone?"

"Yeah. Did you ever bump into Homeless City in your wanderings?"

"I did."

"Well, I don't think it exists anymore."

Lacey said, "It's been a couple of weeks since I was there."

Hanna asked, "There?"

Lacey remarked, "Electronically."

Jack asked, "What were you doing?"

"Snooping. I came across the rumor of it a while back on the dark web, then started hacking around after I became curious if it was real. The places where I frequent were alive with rumors, and hackers I knew were competing to find out stuff about the city. I figured out it was true then found a way to slip into the city's computer systems and I started peeking through their cams. They have cams everywhere, you know, I mean everywhere. I saw some strange things. The city gave me the creeps and reminded me of a huge institution. The people that I followed from the time they arrived seemed dehumanized. It was like they were being warehoused with no real concern about what happened to them. I was surprised at how many cams were placed around that city. It was a voyeur's dream. I saw every private thing you could imagine like meetings with the big shots, some security vids, cells with people locked up, people masturbating and having sex, doctor's exams, large shower rooms, you know private things, then I saw a few women raped in their rooms in the place they called the Asylum. You'd think that these assholes wouldn't pull that crap because everything is recorded but they didn't seem to care. After that, I bugged out. It was just too depressing."

"Hanna and I were living there."

"You? You're not homeless."

"I had needed to go deep underground for a bit."

"Deeper than you already were?"

"Yeah. Colter is trying to find me. He's been more motivated lately."

"Colter, that aaaab."

Hanna said questioningly, “Ab?”

Jack said, “Abnormal. Colter is a sociopath. He has absolutely no conscience.”

“Straight-up fact,” Lacey remarked.

“I’m headed to San Francisco. I’ll need my car if you haven’t sold it.”

Lacey smiled, “I just had a guy coming to see it tomorrow. Damn.”

Jack said, “I need to stay seriously low. After San Francisco, I think I’ll head to Humboldt. I have a cabin deep in the backwoods.”

Lacey said, “Great weed.”

Tiffany smiled.

“If you need any help from me, you let me know.”

“Thanks, Lacey.”

She nodded.

Jack said, “You know me, Lacey. I’m pretty prepared but something happened in Homeless City that no one could prepare for. We barely got out. The people there began to change. They became violent. Their eyes turned white. I think it may have had something to do with something that the government gave them but I’m not sure.”

“Like some kind of experiment?”

“Maybe.”

“White eyes?”

“Yeah.”

Lacey walked to her laptop and typed. A website came up. She clicked her mouse and a video of a female police officer on a street appeared. Lacey put it on full screen. “Look at this. It’s from a cop’s body cam. This happened in Long Beach a couple of days ago. This lady cop was seen on the streets running strangely. She tried to bite the cop who tried to stop her near the morgue. The cop had to shoot her to stop her from attacking him and his partner, but she had the white-eye-thing going on."

"Shit, Hanna. It's outside Homeless City. Shit!"

"What?" Lacey said and could feel the alarm.

"You listen to me, Lacey. You get from here. I've seen people bitten from these white-eyed things. Within seconds they change into them. It's bizarre."

"I don't really want to leave here."

"You still have your place on the Amalfi Coast in Italy?"

"Of course."

"That would be a good place to go. ASAP. Before countries close their borders."

"Jack, you're scaring me. I've never seen you so spooked."

"I am spooked, Lacey, seriously spooked. If this is some kind of virus or something, countries will shut everyone out, especially from the U.S."

"I'll poke around some tonight and see what I can find out."

"Were tired, Lacey. We had to run from Homeless City when the place went batshit crazy. They nuked it, you know."

"What?! I didn't know. I hadn't paid attention to it for weeks."

"It was on the news this morning."

"Oh, I've been busy today," Lacey glanced at Tiffany who smiled angelically.

Jack asked, "We haven't eaten today, got any eggs?"

"Yeah. Let me get you guys a meal. We haven't had dinner either."

"Thanks, Lacey."

Lacey stood and walked to the kitchen.

Tiffany had been rolling another joint. She lit it.

Jack stood to help Lacey and Tiffany sat down close to Hanna, passed her the joint, and smiled at her seductively.

Jack watched and said, "Tiffany seems friendly."

"What can I say, Jack. She's cute, adventurous, uninhibited, and fun."

"And a little younger than your usual."

"Well, I couldn't help myself. By the way, I don't think I could handle another orgasm today. Maybe you and Hanna could occupy her tonight."

"I'd miss you."

"No, you wouldn't, believe me."

"Hanna isn't the sharing type."

Lacey smiled. "Open another bottle of wine for me?"

"Sure."

Lacey commented rhetorically, "The night's young, and Tiffany is, ah, persuasive."

Jack smiled.

Lacey asked, "You leaving in the morning?"

"First light."

"You really think I should hike?"

"You get away from here, Lacey. You get far away. This is going out of control; I can feel it. Fergusson is incompetent to handle a hangnail. He won't do shit. Or by the time he gets around to doing anything, it will be too late."

"He seemed to handle Homeless City."

"Yeah, well, that might not have been him."

"Colter?"

"That would be my guess."

"Geez, Jack."

“He can’t start nuking the entire west coast. Or maybe he can. Whatever, this is going out of control.”

Lacey nodded and flipped the bacon in the pan. She glanced out and could see that Tiffany was reading Hanna’s palm.

Lacey glanced at Jack, nodded towards Tiffany, and said, “That’s how she got into my pants.”

“Maybe I should go out and rescue Hanna.”

“Let’s just watch. If she talks Hanna into a massage, you might lose your lady for the night. Tiffany has magic hands.”

Jack could tell that Hanna was high. He smiled, shrugged, nodded, and said, “Whatever.” He then began cutting honeydew melon into chunks. “I want to continue this discussion. Can I talk in front of Tiffany?”

“Yeah, I wouldn’t mention the government stuff, though, in case she ends up being questioned at some point. The apocalypse stuff is okay.”

Jack nodded.

Tiffany could be overheard saying, “Hum, Hanna. You’re interesting.”

“I am?”

“Oh, yeah.”

“Food’s ready,” Lacey announced.

Hanna stood.

Tiffany stood also but looked a bit disappointed at the timing of the meal.

Lacey plated the food and set it at the table. The four sat eating breakfast food and drinking wine. The weed was strong and everyone was buzzed.

Jack said, “I think everyone but us in Homeless City had become like the guy you saw in the street. I saw people who were dead come back to life. Some were running around naked with toe-tags."

Lacey stopped chewing and glanced up at Jack. "Shit!"

"I know. It was crazy. Somehow, I got to figure out what's going on but from a distance. If one of these things bite you, you become just like them in less than thirty seconds. I saw people with terrible wounds and shot at point-blank range not bothered by their injuries. Their eyes just seemed to lighten at first but soon turned white. They were attacking any human not changed. I saw them savagely attacking people as if to kill them then just stop when the person changed. It didn't make sense and the people attacked were seriously ripped-up but I never saw them attack each other. Then the people that were attacked just joined them."

"Shit, Lacey," Tiffany said, nodding her head towards Jack. "This guy's scary but I really like his friend." She smiled flirtatiously at Hanna then said, "You should let me give you a massage after dinner while the grown-ups chat. I can make you feel like a new woman."

Jack smiled.

Hanna said, "Oh, well, we'll see."

Tiffany continued, wanting to change the subject. She said to Hanna, "You have an interesting palm. You have had many relationships and many of them seem to overlap. You've had bad luck in your life and trouble with allowing anyone close. I think it's because you've mostly been with the wrong kind of man for you." She subconsciously glanced in Jack's direction, then continued, "Maybe it's because you've only been with men." Tiffany smiled and took a bite of her eggs. "After we eat, I'll finish your palm."

Hanna smiled politely and Lacey glanced at Jack.

They finished their meal quietly and all brought their dishes to the sink, rinsed them, and put them in the dishwasher. Lacey washed the pans and Jack dried.

Tiffany walked with Hanna back to the couch and sat close to her then asked, "Can I finish with your palm?"

"I guess," Hanna responded.

Tiffany took Hanna's hand and placed it facing up, then interlocked her fingers with Hanna's. Tiffany closed her eyes and pulled Hanna close pressing her body against Hanna's then pushed back and brushed Hanna's arm from the elbow to the tips of her fingers, caressing her hand. Hanna seemed to oddly melt into Tiffany's touch and embrace as if hypnotized.

Lacey said to Jack, "Tiffany is a clairvoyant. She's connected to some information that no one else seems to know."

Tiffany opened her eyes, brushed the top of Hanna's hand, examined the palm, and began to whisper in Hanna's ear, close to her neck, "Close your eyes and let your mind go blank. Let me in, Hanna. Let me inside of you. Let me be everywhere..."

Hanna could feel Tiffany's breath on her neck.

Tiffany continued, "You are passionate, Hanna. You speak through your body and your sex. Anyone who has been in your intimacy wishes to be back there. Anyone who has had the pleasure of sharing your bed wishes to never leave. There are strings of broken hearts in all directions past but not forward, that I can see. I also saw that you were forced. It seems like at least three times, maybe four, in your life but one was fuzzy."

Hanna's eyes widened in surprise. She turned slightly towards Tiffany and nodded.

"I want to see more," Tiffany said.

Hanna's eyes drooped but she had a slight smile on her face.

Tiffany began to lightly stroke Hanna's thigh. Hanna's legs seemed to involuntarily part.

Tiffany whispered, "Let's do that massage and I'll tell you more of what I know."

Hanna nodded and seemed to beckon the touch.

Tiffany whispered questioningly, "Come with me?"

Hanna nodded again then seemed to wake from the spell and said, "I'm getting a massage, Jack."

Jack smiled and nodded.

***

Tiffany walked Hanna into a back bedroom. Here, Hanna could see a massage table.

"Wow," Hanna remarked. "That looks pretty official."

"I'm a professional masseuse. I take my craft very seriously."

"Oh."

"That's where I first met Lacey. I was working for a chiropractor. She came in for an adjustment and then to my table. Her back was thrashed. Take off all of your clothes and lay face-down. I'll put this towel over your private places."

"I need a quick shower."

"Come with me. I'll get you a towel."

Tiffany walked Hanna across the hall to a large shower that had no commode, a fully tiled floor, and a couple of padded benches. One full wall was mirrored. The shower was not enclosed and had heads that shot out in different directions with rain heads from the ceiling.

Hanna turned from Tiffany and began to undress.

Tiffany said, “No underwear?”

Hanna turned back thinking that Tiffany had left and said, “We literally had to run, Tiffany. Jack wasn’t kidding. I think you need to find a way out of Southern California.”

Tiffany didn’t respond to the comment. She said, “Pretty body, Hanna. You are beautiful.”

“Ah, thanks.”

“Give me your jumpsuit and I’ll carry it into the massage room for you. Wrap up in the towel when you’re finished showering.”

“Okay.”

Hanna showered quickly, wrapped in the towel, and walked into the massage room.

Tiffany smiled and said, “Lay down, put your face in the hole, close your eyes and relax. If you doze, that’s fine. This is a completely safe space.”

“Okay?”

“Don’t worry, Hanna. I’m very serious about my work and I don’t stray from the job. You will come off this table feeling rejuvenated.”

“Okay, so you’re not trying to seduce me?”

“Oh, I’d love to but not before I do what I do with a massage. Besides, you’re not into women sexually. I could see that clearly in your palm... Not that I couldn’t give you some moments of ecstasy.”

Hanna's face remained neutral. She laid and put her face in the hole at the top of the table.

Tiffany then commented, “When I bring someone to my bed, I want them there completely, mind, body, and soul. Sex isn’t as fun if the person isn’t fully in the moment.”

Tiffany laid the towel over Hanna’s backside then lifted it again and brushed at some abrasions.

She said, “You have several cuts and bruises on your bottom and lower back. Your elbows are scraped-up also.”

“Yeah, I fell. I’m pretty sore.”

“I’ll be careful.”

Tiffany laid the towel back over Hanna’s bottom and began with Hanna’s neck. She said, “You’re in knots, Hanna.”

“I’m sure I am.”

Tiffany got down to business then casually commented, “You really like Jack.”

“Yeah. He’s different for me.”

“I could see that,” Tiffany responded as she moved to Hanna’s shoulders. “I could see in my reading that you have been very restless in your life. Many affairs. I’m not judging you on your path. It’s just the journey that you must traverse.”

“It is true. I don’t know how you know that. I have never stayed happy in any relationship. I start happy but then become restless, just like you said.”

“Relax, Hanna, and let your mind be free of any trouble, and I will help your body. No more talking.”

***

Jack finished drying the dishes and helped to clean the counters.

Lacey said, "Let's get out there on the planet and poke around. You got your laptop?"

"Yeah, but I don't want to fire it up here just in case."

"In case what? You've never been tracked."

"In case I might trip some alarm that gives away your location. I think they saw me at Homeless City and I worry that they might follow me here or at least be looking for me in the L.A. area. You know what that means? Cattle prods."

"Got ya. I'd just as soon skip the cattle prods, at least without a safe word."

Jack smiled. He and Lacey had always had good chemistry.

Let me put a couple of files on your machine. It won't give you all the access that I have but it will give you some places around the edges. Good places that you'll enjoy but make sure you bounce off of outside locations."

"Jack. Isn't that what I always do?"

"Just reminding you. These people aren't the kind you're used to running into online. They're not the hacker types, all bark, and no bite. These guys don't play. They have no moral compass. If they catch you, and want something from you, you're toast and it won't be quick."

"I get it," Lacey replied.

"Good."

Jack slipped his flash drive into Lacey's computer and dragged two files onto her desktop.

"Alright," Jack said, sliding out the flash drive and slipping it back into his pocket.

Lacey said, "You wouldn't want to make me a copy of that thing, would you?"

"Sorry. But if I die, I'll will it to you."

"Haha."

"What do you think Hanna and Tiffany are up to in there?"

"Just massage. Want to watch?"

"You have a cam in there. I have cams everywhere. You know hackers. We don't trust anyone and we are the worst of voyeurs."

Lacey typed a command and a picture of Hanna on a massage table appeared. She had a towel over her bottom and looked very relaxed.

"So, no sex play yet?"

"Jack!" Lacey said with raised eyes. "I've never known you to be jealous. Tiffany is very serious about her massages." Lacey slid the picture of the continuing massage to the top of the screen in a small box.

"I'm not jealous. I just thought that the suggestion of a massage seemed a bit sexually charged."

"Tiffany will not give Hanna a massage with a happy ending, at least not the first massage. But Hanna will leave that table feeling incredible. You should let Tiffany give you one also if she asks. She might be tired after Hanna, though."

"I got the impression that her massages were a seduction."

"Oh, they are. You'll leave the table wanting her to touch you more intimately. You'll leave the table nearly begging for it."

"Huh?"

"The second time she gave me a massage, I could feel my body crave the intimacy and I could feel that she knew. It was like she slipped into my desires. That time she brought me over the edge and we've been together ever since."

Tiffany finished with Hanna's feet and raised the towel to have Hanna flip over onto her back. Tiffany glanced up at the camera and half-smiled.

Hanna laid down and Tiffany arranged the towel to cover Hanna's private place though she didn't cover Hanna's breasts.

After seeing Hanna nude, Lacey said, "Very beautiful, Jack. Now I'm the jealous one."

Tiffany went back to work again starting on Hanna's shoulders and neck.

Lacey said, "Let's get to work."

She pulled up several chatrooms at once to see the banter. As usual, they were trashing the President and talking about conspiracy theories. She couldn't find anything having to do with Jack's weird creatures. Then Jack had her use one of the pieces of software that he had put on her computer.

He said, "They must have sent out specimens of these changing things to be analyzed." He then said, "Move over and let me at your keyboard."

Jack glanced at the massage and watched for a second.

Tiffany slid her hands down Hanna's taught stomach. Her thumbs glided under the towel, pushing it down slightly and revealing the light brown tuft of hair below Hanna's navel. Hanna seemed to arch slightly in anticipation of a more intimate touch that didn't occur. Her legs slightly parted. The towel slipped completely off, falling to the ground.

Again, Tiffany glanced at the camera and half-smiled. She walked around and picked up the towel replacing it then continued the massage rubbing the highest portion of Hanna's inner thighs and pushing her thighs farther apart.

Hanna complied and let her legs part even farther, seeming to offer herself to Tiffany.

Tiffany used both hands on each of Hanna's upper thighs. Hanna's breathing increased and could feel her arousal and wanted to guide Tiffany's hands to be more personal.

Tiffany could sense Hanna's arousal and instead of becoming more familiar with her, she moved her hands back across Hanna's stomach, then lightly brushed Hanna's breasts with her fingertips as she moved back towards Hanna's head. She massaged Hanna's shoulders and neck then Hanna's temples and Tiffany whispered, "Rest, Hanna. Let your mind drift into a pleasant sleep."

Hanna could feel her intense arousal ease and her body begin to go slack.

Tiffany whispered, "Rest and when you wake, you'll feel refreshed."

Hanna could feel herself drift further as Tiffany gently massaged Hanna's shoulders and moved back to her arms and hands.

Tiffany softly said, "Rest."

***

Jack went to a site that he knew was monitoring Homeless City. It was probably in the basement at Langley. He'd need to cover his tracks so he redirected his answers to places away from Lacey's IP address. He was looking for one thing, where were any samples sent to?

"Got it," he said triumphantly. "UCLA Medical Center."

He shut down his search and quickly scrubbed his tracks sending anyone attempting to follow all over the world to schools, personal computers, small businesses, and libraries.

"Now," Jack said, "Let's see what they found out."

Jack's fingers danced quickly on the keyboard and he easily hacked into UCLA's database then he began to search.

"Huh?" he said.

"What is it?" Lacey asked.

"I see two cross-referenced specimen samples. One from Homeless City and one, surprisingly, from Edwards Air Force Base. They seem to be from the same person. There are no notes, just two numbers... Now, what did they find?"

Jack pulled up a report and scrolled down to the findings of one female individual. He squinted at the monitor as he read the small print. "Okay. It says that the tiny samples from the lungs on both samples were filled with a microscopic mold. The mold then was found to harbor a virus smaller than any known virus on earth. The virus was so small that they nearly missed it. It was contained inside of the mold and..." Jack paused. "What?" he stopped again...

"What, Jack?"

"They think that the virus wasn't released until this patient had died. Like the death activated the virus."

"That seems counterproductive, that is if you happen to be a virus," Lacey commented.

"Yeah." Jack continued reading down the page, then said, "They think that the way the virus reacted to the cells was possible proof that the person had already died. That in this case, the virus seemed to be attacking the cells postmortem."

Then Jack's eyes raised in shock.

"What is it, now?" Lacey asked.

"These researchers say that some kind of parasite detached from the virus and took over the cells and that after, the parasite seemed to burrow through its own cell and to attach itself to any close-by cell. All the cells studied were connected by a weave of parasites."

"Geez, Jack, what does that mean?"

"I have no idea. I need to think about it."

"Are we finished?"

"Yeah. I need some sleep." Jack rubbed his eyes and was fighting to keep them open. He blinked.

Tiffany walked from the back room and said, "Hanna is snoozing."

"We've had a bad couple of days," Jack said.

"Hanna's a cool person," Tiffany said. "Killer body, though, it's a bit beat up."

"Yeah, it's pretty nice," Lacey agreed.

"Your turn," Tiffany said to Jack.

"I'm beat, too, Tiffany. I'd fall asleep before I got my clothes off."

Lacey said, "You and Hanna can use the room that she's sleeping in. The sheets are fresh and when she wakes, she can crawl in bed with you."

"Thanks, Lacey. I owe you as usual."

"No problem, Jack. You know I love you." She walked up to him and gave him a hug, kissed him on the lips, and patted his butt. "You go to bed with your lady."

"Thanks. We'll see you in the morning."

Jack walked to the room and Hanna was breathing softly and rhythmically as she slept. She was topless on the massage table with her arms at her sides and the towel over her private place.

Jack smiled, took off his clothes, and climbed into bed. He thought about shaking Hanna but she was sleeping so peacefully and the room was warm. An hour later, Hanna woke and crawled in bed with him and they slept...

Chapter 59

Santa Clarita, California

Hanna woke first. The sun was shining through the sheer curtains. She blinked at the brightness. She then leaned over and put her arm over Jack's chest and he woke slightly.

"Morning," he said. "What time is it?"

"Dunno," Hanna said then cracked an eyelid, glancing up. "10."

"Ugh," Jack grunted. He knew he wanted an earlier start.

Hanna snuggled closer to him and let her hand travel down to his private place. She said, "I'm so in the mood."

"Obviously, so am I."

"Tiffany made me so horny last night but then I must have dosed. My body was screaming for her to, well, finish me."

Jack smiled and said, "I'm sure you would have enjoyed that."

"You think so?" Hanna said, climbing on top of Jack and bringing him into her.

He breathed out and whispered, "I do."

"Well, maybe," Hanna said and she began to move with Jack. "I'm certainly enjoying this."

A half-hour later, Jack left the room and saw Lacey reading a newspaper, smoking a cigarette, and drinking coffee.

"Morning, Lacey."

"Hey, Jack. How'd you sleep?"

"Like a baby. Can we use your shower?"

"Of course. Want some company? My shower is big. I've had a few fun parties in there."

"Yeah, I remember a couple. Maybe next time. Where's Tiffany?"

"She's a late riser. She probably won't be up until after 12… Coffee?"

"I'd love some."

"Is Hanna awake?"

"Yeah, she'll be out in a minute."

Hanna walked out, "Good Morning."

"Good morning, Hanna," Lacey said, then, "How was that massage last night?"

Jack handed Hanna a cup of coffee.

"Incredible. Tiffany is magic. I feel so loose this morning. Last night, before the massage, I felt like the prizefighter who didn't win the prize."

"Yeah, she's magic."

"And, I got to admit that her palm reading was kind of shocking. She said things that people just don't know. Strange?"

Lacey smiled, then said, "So, Jack, you missed leaving at first light."

"That's because you got me drunk and high last night."

"Not enough to take advantage of you."

"I wouldn't have been good for anyone last night. I was beat."

"There's a bit of news from the plane crash in Death Valley. It says that it was a training mission and that though it appeared like an atomic explosion, it was really a new high explosive device that they were hoping to test, but that it wasn't radioactive."

"Bull—shit," Jack commented as he finished his coffee.

"I'll make us some breakfast and go wake Tiffany. She'd be upset if you left without getting to say goodbye. She really likes you both. Why don't you both go and shower."

Jack nodded and he and Hanna walked to the shower room. When they opened the door, Tiffany was toweling off.

Jack said, "Oops. Sorry."

Tiffany straightened and smiled. She faced Jack and Hanna completely nude and said, "No worries. I'm not bashful."

Lacey walked in. "There you are," she said to Tiffany.

Tiffany half-smiled, dropped her towel in a hamper, and walked to Lacey, kissing her lips.

Lacey kissed her back and rested her hand on Tiffany's bottom.

Tiffany glanced over her shoulder at Jack and Hanna, smiled, then walked out of the shower room without dressing, followed by Lacey.

Jack and Hanna stripped and showered. When they returned to the front room, Lacey had made French toast, bacon, and eggs. Tiffany, now dressed in shorts, a light tee-shirt, and barefoot, smiled and sipped her coffee.

"God, I love the smell of bacon in the morning," Hanna commented.

Lacey smiled and said, "Come and eat."

Hanna said, "I can't thank you enough for your hospitality. Things haven't been great for me lately."

"You're welcome, Hanna. You can come back here anytime, even without him." Lacey nodded at Jack who laughed.

They sat at the table and ate quietly, finished breakfast, cleaned up the mess, and Jack said, "Let's go out to the garage."

The four walked outside the back door and to Lacey's detached garage. Lacey unlocked the side door and turned on the lights.

The four walked in.

An SUV-type car sat under a car cover.

Jack walked over and pulled the cover off a white Ford Edge. It gleamed in the overhead lights. It looked as though it had just been waxed. He raised the hood and reattached the battery.

Lacey handed Jack the fob and he unlocked the doors. He glanced into the driver's side to check the gas level. He then opened the hatchback and pulled a tarp off of an array of weaponry that any army would be proud of, including a grenade launcher. He recovered the weapons with the tarp.

Hanna said, "Geez, Jack, what were you expecting, full-on anarchy?"

"Pretty much. Once my government decided that they no longer cared about the Constitution, I had the feeling that I'd be fighting myself out of some scrapes, but I was completely unprepared for what happened in Homeless City."

Jack went to a locker and unlocked a combination lock. When the door swung open, the locker had five shelves. Four stacked with ammo and one stacked with cash. He lifted a duffle and piled in the ammo. With effort, he hefted the bag and set it in the back with the tarp-covered weapons then he took another small duffle and put the cash inside.

He turned to Lacey, "I need a new license plate. What do you have?"

"I got several. Where do you want to be from?"

"California."

"Here you go." She handed him a California plate with new tags.

"How about a burner phone? I have access to burners in San Francisco but none here. I had to ditch the one I had."

"I got a couple."

She handed him a box with a container holding an unopened phone.

Jack said, "What do I owe you for these?"

"Really, Jack. I'm insulted."

"Thanks, Lacey. Love ya."

"Awe, you're just using me for my stuff."

"And your meals."

Lacey paused for a minute, then said, "So, Jack, you think everything here is going to shit? I mean, for sure?"

"I'm almost sure. Do you have a piece of paper and a pen?"

Lacey walked to a workbench and lifted a small pad and a dull pencil. She handed them to Jack.

Jack jotted down an address and a small map with three directional changes.

"This is my cabin in Humboldt. If you get in trouble, go there. I'm not sure if I'll be there or not. It's fully self-contained, has about a year's food, and is off the grid." Jack pointed at the small piece of paper,

"This part is a dirt road. There's a key to the cabin in the woodpile by the back door. Don't make any calls from there and don't Google it before you come. Just head there. I'll contact you with the number of this burner when I reach San Francisco. Listen, Lacey, and you too, Tiffany. This sickness spreads fast because the carriers are relentless. You'll want to get out before there's any panic. At that point, it might be too late."

Tiffany's eyes were wide with fear. She said, "I couldn't just pick up and go. I don't have anything, just a beat-up old car."

Hanna walked over to her and took both of her hands. "You need to listen to us, Tiffany. All of this stuff is real. When the time comes, and it won't be long, you need to get out of here."

Hanna hugged her tightly.

As they separated, Hanna held Tiffany's hands until Tiffany nodded. Hanna smiled and dropped her hands.

Jack walked up to Lacey and hugged her.

"Goodbye, Lacey. I don't think I'll be coming back this way again. You need to leave sooner rather than later." They separated and he said, "I'll be in touch."

Lacey nodded.

Jack turned to Tiffany and hugged her, "See you later, Tiffany. I'll take a raincheck on the massage but I will hold you to it. You come to Humboldt also."

She nodded and smiled.

Hanna hugged Lacey then Tiffany again.

Jack asked, "Oh, Tiffany, have you ever ridden a motorcycle?"

"Yeah. I had an old boyfriend who rode."

"The bike's yours if you want it."

Her eyes raised in surprise, "Okay, thanks."

He tossed her the key.

Lacey pushed a button on the wall and the garage door began to roll up.

Jack and Hanna climbed into his SUV. Jack started the car and slowly rolled backward. He rolled down his window and said, "You know where to find me, Lacey. Love ya."

"Love ya, too, Jack."

He turned onto the street and he and Hanna waved at Lacey and Tiffany.

They were standing together and Lacey's arm was around Tiffany. They waved back.

As Jack drove off, he said, "I think you'll love the mountains."

Hanna smiled and nodded.

Chapter 60

Langley, Virginia

Atwood Colter received a copy of the reports from the UCLA Medical Center, forwarded from Edwards Air Force Base where they were first sent. He hastily read the report. It was worse than he had thought. He dropped the report onto his desk and stared into space.

He hadn't spoken to President Fergusson for a couple of days. This wouldn't be good news for the President. He was hoping that being able to let Fergusson know that there were no survivors anywhere around Homeless City would be good news but the report was frightening. Hopefully, the mold died in the intense radiation from the explosion.

He glanced again at the report.

On the first sample: "Postmortem, the mold spores release a virus that is infected by a parasite. The virus, at an undetermined point, invades all the cells. Then the parasite emerges from the virus and seems to burrow into the adjacent cells. Once the parasite inhabits the cells, the cells do not seem to deteriorate the way cells normally do in a deceased body."

From the second sample: "The person seemed to be infected by being bitten by someone with active virus. This person's cells were rapidly infected. The parasites were also observed in each of the infected cells in the sample."

Colter stood, stepped from his desk, and headed to the White House.

When he arrived, President Fergusson was watching one of his favorite news reporters explaining how the President had managed to transform the American economy back into the envy of the world.

Colter entered the room and Fergusson said, "Shh, shh. I want to hear this." He waved his hand for Colter to come in and sit down.

"... Then, with the economy beginning to fail, the President instructed Congress to spend a trillion dollars on programs to bolster the Economy. The country was headed to disaster but the President acted quickly and decisively to head off a certain depression."

Fergusson sat back in his chair and beamed. He said, "Now, that's the kind of story that the country needs to hear."

"Yes, Sir," Colter responded flatly.

"So, what is it, Atwood?"

"I have been over all of the film related to the explosion in Homeless City. There are no survivors. We combed the entire desert with drones and every living thing in a twenty-five-mile radius from the center of the city is dead. And I mean everything. We've sent in teams to the edges of the radius of the blast and the area has been sterilized. The radiation is still thick there and continues to kill anything, not in a hazmat suit. We couldn't even bring out the drones because they were too hot."

"So, we're safe from whatever happened."

“I think so, but I just received the report from the UCLA Medical Center that did the analysis of the lung and tissue samples sent from the Homeless City residents that we abducted.”

“Yes, and?”

“It’s scary. The lungs were coated with a kind of mold. The mold is a new discovery. No one could place it and no one had ever seen it before. When a person dies the mold spores hatch, for lack of a better word, and release a virus. Again, this is an entirely new type of virus, smaller than any virus currently known. It was almost missed. It quickly spreads through the dead body jumping from cell to cell. The second sample was from a person who hadn’t died. Somehow, that person became infected with the virus. The report speculated that the person may have become infected from a bite from another infected person. The virus was then believed to do the same thing it did with the first deceased person, rapidly spreading throughout the body.”

“Okay, so what? We killed the virus and the mold with our nuke.”

“Maybe, but that isn’t all. Once the virus infects the cells in the body of the person, then it appears that the parasites take over the body’s cells, connecting them and keeping them somewhat alive which seems to allow them to control the infected person. Then the person becomes a slave to the parasites. There are some known viruses and parasites that do the same thing to animals and insects by controlling certain aspects of their wants and needs but this is a total usurping of the individual.”

“Well, the mold is dead and so are the people who went crazy.”

"Yeah, but where did the mold come from, and did any of it escape the confines of the explosion?"

"I'm not going to be bothered by what-ifs. And, you get this straight, I am not going to alarm the American people. I just got those idiots back to work and the economy expanding again. I don't want anything to mess that up. You can go, Colter," Fergusson said rudely, dismissing him.

"Yes, Sir."

The End

Pathogen Z ...

Safe for now, Jack and Hanna leave Southern California and head to San Francisco. The mold, however, that first appeared at the construction site near Homeless City has begun to spread and anyone who has been exposed to it, and who passes away, comes back to life as something not natural to this world. Then anyone bitten by these creatures changes as the virus and parasites quickly invade all their living cells causing small outbreaks of madness in several American states and Mexico.

The second novel in the *Z Plague* Series, ***"Pathogen: Z,"*** begins...

Other Books by D.R. Swan

<u>The Artifact Series</u>:

Science fiction that revolves around the discovery of an artificially intelligent artifact buried in a hundred-million-year-old dinosaur dig site. The artifact reveals a dire warning and the race is on to save Earth.

Artifact
Waves on Mars
The Coming Storm
Mars, The 51st State

The Sideways Series:

A post-apocalyptic, alien contact series where the "Law of Unintended Consequences" comes into play. The series contains elements of science fiction, romance, pandemic, and magical realism.

Sideways
The Gift
Witch
Shadows
In-Between
Aftermath
The Crystal Circle

The Shapes in the Clouds Series:

This young adult series revolves around Lisa Hyde, a second-year college art student who has gifts that allow her brief glimpses into the future. She soon finds out that the world is far stranger than even she could have imagined. This series contains elements of the paranormal, clairvoyance, romance, magical realism, vampires, and shape-shifters.

Shapes in the Clouds
Dark Knowledge
Feeders Shifters Faders

Two Single Stories:

A Hero's Path

Eleven-year-old Alice discovers an odd book in the attic of an old house that is strange. As she reads it, she finds that the girl in the story is much like her, even with her first name and wearing her clothes but the similarities do not stop there. The girl in the book is on a quest. Alice soon finds that she is also on the quest and must finish the book and she believes that the survival of humanity depends on her decisions.

Reality Augmented

While playing an augmented reality game, Pokémon Go, on a cell phone, four kids are led by the game to an unexpected location with an equally unexpected surprise.

Printed in Great Britain
by Amazon

67740673R00180